SONATA

RISHIRE YOUNG

Hollis House

Copyright © 2024 by Rishire Young.

All rights reserved. No part of this publication may be reproduced, distributed or transmitted in any form or by any means, including photocopying, recording, or other electronic or mechanical methods, without the prior written permission of the publisher, except in the case of brief quotations embodied in critical reviews and certain other noncommercial uses permitted by copyright law. For permission requests, write to the publisher, addressed "Attention: Permissions Coordinator," at the address below.

Hollis House, LLC
www.hollis.house

Publisher's Note: This is a work of fiction. Names, characters, places, and incidents are a product of the author's imagination. Locales and public names are sometimes used for atmospheric purposes. Any resemblance to actual people, living or dead, or to businesses, companies, events, institutions, or locales is completely coincidental.

Book Layout ©2024 BookDesignTemplates.com

Sonata / Rishire Young. -- 1st ed.

RISHIRE YOUNG

SONATA

*For my mother, Christina, and my twin sister,
Marcushire*

My angels

CHAPTER ONE

I feel like my eyes are drowning in a pool that's half-full. Half-full...talk about depressed optimism. I tilt my head back, sucking the tears back where they belong, deep inside, where no one can see them. My red, puffy eyes are dead giveaways that I've been crying, though. Stupid windows to the soul. I sigh, gathering my books, my tongue heavy from the hours of silence. I sigh again, trying to wake it up.

Jordan turns to look at me as I shove books into my bag. I don't see her yet, but I can feel her eyes searching for my face. I rearrange the books in my bag till she looks away. She straightens her bag straps on her shoulders and continues to stare at me. I continue to ignore her, my resolve soon beating hers. She gives me one last look before turning and heading for her next class. Jordan, zero; me, one. I've been winning this battle for the past six months. She still hasn't stopped fighting, though. Poor girl.

I squeeze my eyes shut, checking to see if there are any residual tears left. I'm dry, but my eyes are so heavy I just want to keep them closed. I sit back in my chair and let my head hit the desk with a soft thud. After what feels like an hour, someone taps on my shoulder. I sit up, eyes still closed but facing the tapper.

"Miss Donner, are you alright?" My eyes blink open, and Mrs. Kits is looking down at me through her bifocals, perched low on her nose. She bends her knees and positions herself right in front of my face. I exhale audibly in response. "Nita Beth, I think you should go to the counselor's office." Her voice is soft, like a marshmallow, and almost makes me start crying again.

I nod slowly, although the last thing I want to do is go to the counselor's office. I'm not about to tell Mrs. Kits that, though, so I lift my bag back to my shoulders and drag myself out of the classroom. My feet feel like lead as I make my way to the counselor's office. The hallway is empty. Everyone is either in class or avoiding me like the plague that I am. I've stopped caring about everyone else. The counselor is

Sonata

standing outside her office, looking down the hall at me as I approach.

"Nita Beth Donner," she sings as I get closer.

I slow down, considering all of the possible exit strategies. I could turn and run. I could throw my bag at her then turn and run. I could swiftly turn the corner and walk out. I could fake an emergency phone call. That last thought pushes me forward. I need this counseling. Maybe her too-sweet-for-Willy-Wonka attitude will rub off on me. It hasn't yet, but there's still hope.

"Please take a seat on the couch, or lie down if it makes you more comfortable." Mrs. Miskole sits behind her desk and motions to the couch with her arm like she's Vanna White. I shuffle toward the chair next to the couch and sit down heavily, my body landing like a sack of potatoes. "Okay then..." She scribbles furiously in her notepad. I look down. I don't like watching her take notes on me. It makes me feel like a lab rat or some science experiment. I hope she's actually doodling.

"So, what brings you to my office? I can't imagine you came here of your own volition unless you had a breakthrough. Did you have a breakthrough?!" She clasps her hands together and leans forward, her whole upper body practically splayed on the desk. I lean back, pressing my spine into the chair until our spines become one.

Crossing my legs, I shake my head in response. "Nope. No breakthrough here. I'm probably closer to a breakdown than a breakthrough; at least that's what Mrs. Kits thinks. She sent me." I shrug, crossing my arms over my chest nonchalantly.

"Oh..." I watch her deflate, her body sliding back into the chair. She scribbles again in her notepad, shaking her head. I roll my eyes and exhale through my teeth. "So, what's going on? Why so close to a breakdown?"

I grip the arms of the chair, my fingers digging into the cushion. I hate talking about my feelings or what I've "gone through". Can't the news coverage be enough? Do I have to rehash every painful detail every time I come here? Now I remember why I wanted to run.

"Miss Donner, are you okay?" Mrs. Miskole has her head cocked to the side in her I'm-so-concerned-please-open-up-to-me way. I mirror her head tilt, squint my eyes, and pinch my chin in a pensive way. She laughs shortly. "Miss Donner, you're already here; you might as well talk." Sometimes she makes good points.

Sonata

I throw up my arms and sigh loudly. "Fine! Well it's been six months since the accident, but sometimes it feels like it happened yesterday. This morning I woke up to the scent of chocolate chip pancakes - her signature dish - only to find that my dad had ordered some from IHOP in commemoration. I thought I was going to pass out, I was breathing so hard. Of course I didn't eat the pancakes, so now I'm freaking starving. I'm beyond exhausted, since I've practically stopped sleeping, and I feel like I've lost all cognition of my body's movements. This is all to say that I miss my mom. I miss my mom, okay! Have I broken through yet?!"

I'm fuming now. I can't believe this woman is talking to me like she doesn't know my story. I'm so done with this! I push myself out of the chair forcefully, it's legs scraping at the floor, leaving the faintest mark.

"Nita Beth, wait!" Mrs. Miskole is at the door before I can get my backpack on. "This is a technique, a counseling technique. I have to gauge your awareness of the situation and make sure you're still acknowledging your pain."

"Next time, to save time, can you just assume I'm in tune with my emotions?" I feel deflated, like when you're blowing up a balloon but you lose your grip so all the air seeps out in a rush then slowly as it gets emptier. In my head, I'm lying limp on the floor, an empty balloon.

She rubs her eyes and puts her hand on her hip in resignation. "Yes, fine, deal. Now will you please sit down?" I bend my knees about to oblige. The bell rings just as my butt grazes the seat cushion. I wobble as I try to stand again without sitting first. I grab hold of the arms of the chair and push myself up. I tip an invisible hat to Mrs. Miskole and shrug my backpack on.

"Saved by the bell." I swing out into the hallway happy to be free from that useless conversation.

I stride down the hall toward my locker, my face stuck in a smug expression as I ruminate on my witty, if not clichéd, farewell. Classrooms vomit out crowds of students, all talking in their outside voices about something or other. I block it all out, creating my own mental bubble where I'm free from the inane chatter of my so-called peers. I'm blocking everything out so successfully that I actually run into Jordan. Our heads smack together, and I bounce off her and onto the floor.

"My gosh!" I feel my head for the bump that I know is starting to form. Jordan reaches down, taking a hold of my arm. I shake her off violently. "I'm fine." I

Sonata

push myself up and straighten my bag. Brushing off my pants, I look up at Jordan through my eyelashes.

"Oh my gosh, Nita! I'm so sorry!"

"NBD," I say, fighting the smile associated with our old joke. My initials sure do make for an often relevant acronym. "Did you need something?" I start walking before she can speak. She's on my heels, trying to catch up as I practically jog away.

"I just wanted to check on you. You weren't in history class, so I hoped you were at Mrs. Miskole's office."

"You must be a psychic. That's exactly where I was." I get to my locker and open it so that it almost hits her in the face. She steps back quickly, narrowly avoiding the door. "Was that all?" I'm not looking for round two with Jordan. I just want to get today over with.

She moves to lean on the locker next to mine, facing me as I shove my bag into my locker. "NB, why are you avoiding me? I want to help you." I turn to her abruptly, my hair slapping her in the face as I knew it would.

"Help me? What makes you think you can do that? What makes you think I need help?"

Somewhat undeterred, she puts her hand on my shoulder and tilts her head to the side like Mrs.

Miskole. "I know it was six months ago today that it happened. I can see that you're having a tough day. Let me be there for you." I shrug her hand off.

"I'd rather be alone." I look down at my shoes and turn my toes toward each other.

"You should've skipped school today. It's really not a good day for you, is it?"

"I would've loved to skip school today, but you know my dad. He thought being around people would help me forget what day it is. Like going on business as usual will make me think it's all business as usual."

"Forget him! Let's get out of here." I raise my eyebrows and lean on my locker.

"Are you really suggesting we both skip class? Like you and me. Leave school before it ends. Do something unrelated to our education."

Jordan is what you would call a classic nerd. She loves school and everything having to do with school. It's amazing that we're friends, considering how much of a typical teenager I am when it comes to school -- I could take it or leave it but would prefer to leave it. Ours is a tale as old as time, though. Our parents were friends, and we lived down the street from each other, so one thing led to another, another cliche phrase here, another cliche phrase there, bing bang boom, we became friends. I never really connected with anyone at school, because I would rather just get the whole day over with and make it home to not give it a second thought, but Jordan was so ingrained in my home life, it just made sense that she would be a part of my school life too.

Slowly but surely she invaded my heart. As I learned more about her, I started to actually like her - the way she would wiggle her nose as she tried to solve a complicated problem, her laugh that was more like a bray than anything else, how she knew just when to get close and when to stay away. She has been like the sister I always wanted, and I loved her as such.

In all the years that I've known Jordan she has never once suggested that we do something contrary to what we're supposed to do. Even if a rule was merely implied, she would insist that we follow it thoroughly. She always made sure I did my schoolwork and that I actually took notes in class. Before every test, quiz or exam, she would camp out in my room and force me to study. She single-handedly has kept me from failing out, and I have kept her from eating lunch alone. I make sure she's not all work and no play, and she makes sure that I'm not all play and no work. We balance each other out.

She nods her head conspiratorially, a sly smile sliding across her face. "That's exactly what I'm saying."

I slam my locker shut and turn back to her. "Well alright, Jordan 2.0. Let's hit it!"

We stride toward the nearest exit. Jordan tries to slip her arm into mine, but I shake her off. I guess a little original Jordan has snuck its way into Jordan 2.0. I'll let her touchy-feely-ness slide. I'm getting out of here!

We burst out of the door, laughing a little as the door clangs shut behind us. The sun is high in the sky and lightly kissing my exposed arms. I stop before we reach the parking lot, standing in the grass and letting the sunshine wash over my face. My eyes start to sting as the tears force their way out of their ducts. In this moment I feel so light and so heavy at the same time. The stress of school has washed away, but my mind is too free to think, too free to feel, and too free to remember how broken I am.

My body crumbles to the floor, and I land face down in the soft grass. The blades absorb my tears, but my sobs ring out over the parking lot. Jordan kneels next to me, rubbing my back and stroking my hair. She's whispering, "Shhh, Nita, shhh. It's alright. Let it out." And I do. I let it all out. My sobs become moans as my body shakes. My heart physically hurts, the pain branching off into the rest of my body. I grab at the grass, ripping it out and squeezing the chunks like stress balls. I can tell that I'm about to pass out, and I'm scared. I try to hold on to consciousness, but my body is too tired. I'm too tired.

I release the grass and let out a long breath. My body flattens to the ground, and I feel boneless. I drift off to sleep with Jordan's voice in my ear, sounding just like my mother's.

"Good girl. It's going to be okay..."

"Mom! Dad! I'm home!" I throw my bag onto the couch and run to the kitchen. I grab an apple and bite into it, the juice running down my chin. Wiping it off with the back of my hand, I run back to the living room, scooping up my bag, and bounding up the stairs.

I jump onto the landing, causing the lamp on the table to shake. I walk to my room and notice that the door is wide open. I never leave my door open... Tiptoeing like a sleuth, I peek into my room.

"Dad!" I bounce into the room and toss my bag onto the floor. My dad is sitting on my bed, staring blankly at my wall of photos. I stand next to him, putting one hand on his shoulder and waving the other hand in front of his face. "Dad..." I snap my fingers, causing him to blink. Tears start

flowing down his face, his expression still blank. "Dad!" I sit next to him, hugging him from the side. "What's wrong? Should I get mom?"

As if waking up from hypnosis, he jerks his head toward me and envelopes me with his arms. "Sweetie, I'm so sorry. I'm so sorry. I'm so sorry." He's talking into my hair, his words muffled. I lean back, searching his face for an answer to a question I don't want to ask. "Your mother..." The tears choke him, and he starts to cough.

"Was her flight delayed?" Even as I say it, I know that isn't it. My eyes well up as my body catches up with my mind.

My dad is talking, but I can't hear him anymore. I can't hear him as he tells me that she's gone, that her plane went down and that she's never coming home. The room is spinning, and I have to lie down. He's crying, and he's talking, and I don't think he's here anymore, with me, in my room. I'm not here anymore. We're floating in this moment as our world is ending. The building is crumbling around us, but it's not real. It's not real. It can't be...

I blink rapidly, my eyes having a tough time adjusting to the sun. Jordan has turned me over so that I'm lying on my back. She's holding my hand and forming little circles on the back of it with her thumb. I sigh, causing her to look at me. I blink slowly, watching her as she watches me.

"I guess your dad was right." I laugh despite myself.

"Well there's a first time for everything." I push myself up into a sitting position and turn toward the school. "How long was I out for?"

Jordan looks at her watch. "About five minutes."

"It felt like forever," I whisper. My heart is still trying to beat its way out of my chest, but I feel better. "I guess you want to go back."

As I start to stand, Jordan stays put. "I think we should just sit here till the last bell. What do you think?"

I settle back beside her, allowing her to put her arm around my shoulders and lean her head on mine. I close my eyes and inhale deeply. It smells like freshly cut grass. I hold my breath so nothing can disrupt the scent. The wind blows, causing loose flowers to float around me. I feel like I'm in a princess movie, and I can talk to tailoring animals. If only I could transport myself by thought.

Jordan shifts at my side. I open my eyes to see her punching her thigh. She looks at me with a small smile. "Leg fell asleep."

Rishire Young

I laugh, willing to let the moment and the sadness of this day pass so that I can really appreciate my friend. I stand up and hold my hand out to her. She grabs it, and I jerk her up.

"Let's go for a walk." I put my arm around her shoulders, something I haven't done in a while. Her shoulders raise, and I can tell she's fighting to hold back a squeal. We walk around the parking lot, our silence peaceful and not awkward. As we reach my car, I bump her hip with my own and let my arm fall back to my side. She turns to me and smiles, her eyes saying everything she wants to say. I smile back, trying to imitate her radiance.

In my back pocket, my phone vibrates. I check the caller ID, and my heart stops. Dad. I look at Jordan, my mouth agape and my face drained of almost all color, a considerable feat considering my dark complexion. She grabs my hand and squeezes, the pressure relieving some of my own. I inhale deeply and exhale loudly. Sliding my finger across the bottom of my phone, I bring it to my ear, my hand shaking so much I'm afraid I'm going to drop it.

"Dad?" My voice cracks, and my eyes take that as a cue to well up again.

"Honey, are you okay?" He sounds just as panicked as I feel.

Sonata

"Are you?" I keep my eyes locked on Jordan's to stay grounded.

"Sweetie, I'm fine. I was just calling to see how your day is going. I got a call from the guidance counselor, and she said you may be having a rough one. I figured I'd catch you on a break."

I let go of the breath I didn't realize I was holding. I squeeze Jordan's hand then let go.

"I'm actually going to head home right now, so I'll talk to you when I get there."

"Maybe you should take a minute to gather yourself." He's laughing through the sentence, but I can tell he's really worried. I nod even though I know he can't see me. Hanging up, I can't help but smile, I feel so relieved. I look at Jordan, and I try to laugh. The worry hasn't worn off, so all I can muster is a smile and a reassuring hand on her shoulder.

"My dad is such a nut. He wants me to come home." She's not smiling back, so I smile even wider, allowing the grin to reach my eyes so she knows it's for real. "Everything's fine. I'm going to head home."

I jerk back the door handle, causing the door to swing open. She holds onto it with both hands as I slide into the driver's seat. I buckle my seatbelt and start the engine. She's still holding onto the door, the look of worry still pasted on her face. I reach my hand up and pry her fingers off the door. She laughs a little, some of the tension releasing with each finger I pry off. She pushes the door so it slams shut and leans forward, her face almost pressed against the window. I roll it down and stick my arm out to pat her on the shoulder.

"Call me when you get home?"

"J, it's twenty minutes away." I squeeze her shoulder and place my hands at ten and two on the steering wheel.

She reaches into the car and pulls at my earlobe. I turn my head quickly, practically giving myself whiplash. Her pleading gaze furrows my eyebrows. "Please?" Sighing, I nod and put the car in reverse, almost running over her toes.

As I drive home, I can't help but be kind of annoyed at the level of concern a simple phone call can elicit. I was so scared that something bad had happened to my dad that I almost threw up. Jordan was acting like a parent whose only child just started driving. I feel like everything I do now has a silhouette of fear over it. Just waking up is a death wish. My drive home, which is usually peaceful and calming, the rare moment of me-time when I can just chill, is now an action-packed thriller with invisible dangers that could take me at any moment. I try to calm down, but every movement makes me jump out of my skin.

Sonata

I turn up the volume on the radio and feel my nerves unwinding. Singing at the top of my lungs, I can almost forget how terrified I am. Within minutes I'm in my driveway, and I can put the whole car ride behind me. I turn the key, switching off the ignition, and gather my things in my left arm. I slam the car door shut, hoping the noise will bring my dad to the front door. Walking toward the house, I can't help but feel a sense of déjà vu.

CHAPTER TWO

My key slides effortlessly into the door, but the door doesn't budge. "Dad!" I'm pushing against the door with all my strength, but I'm getting nowhere. "Dad!" I'm tired, and this is quickly getting annoying.

I can hear footsteps on the other side. The sound of heavy shuffling and shoving is met with the swinging of the door. "Welcome home, Sweetie!"

I move past my dad and his outstretched arms into our foyer that's covered in boxes. "Did you become a hoarder while I was at school?" I lightly kick the nearest box, growing more and more curious.

Dad puts his arm around my shoulders and tousles my hair. "Very funny, little girl. This is stuff from the basement." I bend down to get a better look at the boxes. "Your mother's stuff..." He trails off as I straighten up, my back stiff with anger; I turn to the

Sonata

stairs and jog up to my room without saying a word. As soon as I get there, I slam the door.

I can't believe he thought it would be okay to just shove all this nostalgic stuff in my face on the anniversary of all days! It's like he has no concept of grieving or how hard this has been for me. Sure, I put up a strong front, and I'm rocking a stiff upper lip, but he's my dad; he should see that I'm crumbling inside. First, he makes me go to school, and now this! It's like he's trying to make this the hardest day ever.

"Sweetie?" He knocks a rhythm on my door. I flop onto my bed and bury my head in my pillow. I hear the door creak open slowly. I remain buried in my pillow. "I'm so..." I can feel his hand hovering above my back. "...sorry." He doesn't pat me but instead puts something on my bedside table and leaves, clicking the door shut behind him.

I keep my head down for another minute although I'm practically suffocating - I like the way it feels. I reach my hand out to the bedside table and feel for the thing he left. My fingers connect with a familiar glass dome, and my head pops up. Mimicking a sun salutation, I crane my neck to stare at the thing. It's a snow globe. My eyes water, and suddenly I'm lost in a memory.

"Nita, honey, it's alright!" Mom strokes my hair as she lowers herself onto my bed. "Everything is alright," she whispers. "I'm here. I've got you."

I lean into her, sighing heavily. My face is streaked with tears and soaked in sweat. I shiver despite the warmth. Mom wraps her arms around my body and brings me closer. I wipe my dripping nose and subtly rub the snot into the fabric of Mom's nightshirt. She laughs and hands me a tissue from my bedside table. I guess I wasn't that subtle.

"Do you want to talk about it?" I shake my head, blowing my nose so hard I'm sure some of my brain comes out.

I couldn't talk about it even if I wanted to. This nightmare came out of nowhere and left with the same swiftness, my sadness the only memory. She laughs again and reaches over to the side of the bed.

"I thought this would help." She puts a snow globe on her lap and turns the winding key. The beginning strains of Beethoven's Piano Sonata No. 14 fill the room.

I'm already falling asleep. I reach out and touch the glass dome of the snow globe. I can barely make out the Rockefeller Center Ice Rink within. My eyelids are heavy, but before I'm completely gone, I take my mother's hand. "I love you, Mom."

She squeezes my fingers then lets my hand rest on my bed. "I love you, too."

Sonata

I reach for the snow globe and trace the line of the dome with the tip of my finger. I pick it up and bring it close to my face. Everything looks like it did two years ago when I thought I lost it. Nothing has changed and yet so much is different.

I twist the winding key and put it back on my bedside table. Fully clothed, I get under my blanket and close my eyes as my head hits the pillow. Beethoven's Piano Sonata No. 14 fills the room, and I'm gone just like before.

The sun sneaks through the blinds and forces its way behind my eyelids. I groan and put my hand over my eyes. I don't know what time it is, but I know it's too early for me to wake up. I flip onto my face and put a pillow over my head. I start to fall back asleep, but the sound of my bedroom door opening keeps me alert. I wait for my dad to say something, but what I hear shocks me upright.

"Nita Beth, wake up!" My mom bounces onto my bed and jumps on her knees, shaking me almost onto the floor. "Don't you see it's a beautiful day? We have to take a walk, we just have to!"

I can barely breathe. My mind is spinning, and I have to hold onto my bedside table to keep steady. I start to hyperventilate, and my mom grabs my hand.

"Honey, what's wrong? Are you okay? What's going on?" She's next to me now, rubbing concentric circles into my back. "Come on, honey, breathe. Inhale, exhale, repeat. Come on." She looks comical breathing so ostensibly - like someone helping a pregnant woman through labor. I laugh, the moment too unreal not to be funny. "There you go!" She pinches my cheek and laughs with me.

I still don't know what's going on. Am I dreaming? I don't feel like I'm dreaming. Is this what dreaming feels like?! What should I do? Just go with it? I might as well; this is everything I've wanted for the past six months. If this is a dream, here's hoping I don't wake up soon.

"So, about that walk?" I jump out of my bed and stretch like a cat. "Where do you want to go?"

My mom claps her hands and joins me beside my bed. She shakes me by the shoulders then gives them a tight squeeze. "How about that park by Hickory Smalt Circle?"

I shimmy on a pair of denim shorts and adjust the straps of my tank top. Slipping my feet into a pair of flip flops, I grab my bag and slap my mom on the butt. "Let's go!" She laughs and chases me down the stairs.

Grabbing my keys off the side table, I notice my dad isn't around. I go into the kitchen, into the living room, and back upstairs into my parents' room, and I still can't find him. Bounding back downstairs, I'm surprised by how little I care. It's not that I don't care about my dad. This is just a dream, so why worry, right? I'll see him when I wake up.

I find my mom standing in the doorway. She has her hand on her hip and a pout on her lips, waiting for me. I laugh and pull her out into the yard. We walk arm-in-arm down the street toward Hickory Smalt Circle. I rest my head on her shoulder, taking in everything I can before I wake up. I don't want to wake up. I'm keeping my eyes open so much that they're drying out.

"What are you doing?" My mom is looking down at me, causing us to walk off the sidewalk. "Oh!" She trips a bit and pulls me down to the ground.

"Mom!" I laugh as I land in the grass beside her.

Rishire Young

"Don't you 'mom' me! I was just checking on you. You made me trip!" She pokes me in the side, her finger feeling like a sharp object. I hold my breath, hoping the pain won't wake me up. Blinking slowly, I reach out for my mom to make sure she's still there. She playfully brushes my hand off. "Okay, handsy!" I pinch her shoulder and stand, extending my hand out to her. She gets on one knee and takes my hand. "Nita Beth Donner, will you marry me?"

I laugh and push her down. She lands on her butt, her face in a fake scowl. She stands and swipes at her backside. Punching me lightly on the arm, she smiles the smile I've missed so much. I stop in my tracks and stare at her, my eyes filling with tears I didn't know I was holding back. "Mom..."

She looks down at me, eyebrows furrowed, forehead wrinkled. "What's going on, honey? Why do you keep looking at me like you can't believe I'm here?"

Would admitting that I know I'm in a dream make the dream end? To my left, a bird springs off the ground and darts toward a nearby tree. As the bird lands on the tree, it clears, dozens of birds emptying out of the tree in a hurry. Squirrels run down the tree and a cluster of mosquitoes gather around the branches. A quiet breeze moves in front of my face, entering my ears like a whisper. The moment lasts an eternity,

Sonata

and although we're just standing there, staring at each other, I never want it to end. I don't want to mess this up.

I reach up and put her hair behind her ear. I pat her on the cheek and only let half of my mouth smile. "You just look so pretty today. Is it illegal to stare?"

She pushes me for the hundredth time since I woke up. "You're ridiculous. Come on."

When we finally make our way to the park, the sun has moved down so low that it's almost hidden by the far off mountains. The breeze has picked up, and it's starting to get chilly. Leaves dance through the sky to a song only they can hear. My mom jumps through them, disrupting their tango and getting leaves caught in her hair. Her laugh sounds like a child's. She dances around the park, uninhibited, and all I can do is stare at her. All I had ever done was stare at her. Watching her now brings it all back, and it's almost too much to take. There's a ringing in my ears, and I know I'm about to pass out. I reach out my hand and call out in a voice that comes out as a whisper.

"Mom."

I wake up enshrouded in blankets. Blinking slowly, I arch my back and wiggle my way out of my cocoon. Suddenly I remember where I was, where I want to be. I sit upright and notice that I'm in my room. The curtains are drawn, creating the appearance of nightfall, but on my bedside table the clock reads 5:30 pm.

I'm still wondering when I am. Everything looks like it should, my room looks the same when I'm both awake and asleep, so that doesn't help anything. I want to go outside and check if my mom is still there, but I'm too nervous that she'll be gone again in a permanent way that is somehow harder than before after having just spent the day with her.

Now the clock reads 6 pm. I haven't moved; I feel glued to my bed. I release the tension in my back that has been keeping me upright this whole time and fall back onto my bed with a small bounce. I pull the covers over my face and shut my eyes as tight as I can. I'm trying to fall asleep, but my mind won't shut up. I can't stop wondering how the world works. If I fall asleep in my dream, where will I end up?

My ears start to itch in the hardest to reach place, that little hole where people shove Q-tips. I ignore it and stick my hands between my butt and the bed, rendering myself nearly immobile. My eyes fly open at the sound of a knock on my door. I stay under the covers, the suspense making me itch all over as footsteps creep closer and closer to my bedside. I can tell that whoever is here is kneeling beside my head. I'm

Sonata

too scared to move. Is it weird that I'm too scared to move?

"Honey?" I throw the covers off of me and wrap my arms around my mom.

"I'm so glad it's you," I whisper into her hair.

"Who else would it be?" She pats me on the back, laughing into my ear.

I sigh and let my arms drop. "Sorry, just a bad dream. Some horror movie reboot where I'm the star." I laugh and lean into my headboard. She reaches over to run her fingers through my hair, stopping to press a small bump that has formed on my head.

I flick her hand away. "Hey, that's not a button!" I finger the bump. "What happened?"

Mom scoots her way into my bed, pushing me to the other side. "Well, clumsy-pants, you fainted. It was weird; one minute I was dancing with the leaves, the next minute, you're on the floor, napping."

I laugh and nod. "Sounds about right. The floor at the park does look quite comfortable."

She laughs and sinks into my bed. I lay down next to her, as close as I can, so close that her heartbeat feels like mine. Stroking my hair, she hums above my head, a song I don't know but am quickly learning the melody to. I feel like I'm about to fall asleep, but I can't. I have to stay awake; I have to stay in this moment, in this embrace, and I have no idea where sleep will take me. I'm concentrating on staying awake so hard that my fists clench.

"Honey, are you alright?" My mom's hand is on mine, and she's trying to pry my fingers loose. "Come on, loosen up. I'm tired; let's sleep."

She turns away from me and reaches for something on my bedside table. I can't see what she's doing, the weight of her body keeping me trapped under the covers. I can hear the clicking of a winding key turning, but I'm honestly too tired to think, too concentrated on the task at hand – staying awake. As she rolls over, the beginning strains of Beethoven's Piano Sonata No. 14 fills the air. My voice gets caught in my throat as I try to ask her to shut it off. The snow globe is like magic, carrying me away into an alternate night.

CHAPTER THREE

Living in a dream within a dream will have me all sorts of upside down. That's what I'm thinking when I wake up. I'm a little emotionally exhausted at this point. I don't have the mental wherewithal to stay scared. As my eyes open, I reach my arms toward the ceiling, stretching so hard that I think my arms might come out of their sockets. Before I can fully open my eyes, I'm blinded by the ugliest fluorescent lights. I'm sure I look terrible under these circumstances, especially considering I'm wearing some sort of paper gown. I blink about a hundred times, but the lights only get worse. I let out a small groan. Where am I?

"Nita?" I whip my head to my right. "You're awake." My dad reaches toward me from the chair he's sitting in.

Rishire Young

I slink away slightly, unsure of what's going on. My eyes are as wide as they can get. I probably look like a Bratz doll. I can't stop breathing through my mouth like a dog after a fierce game of fetch. My dad is out of his chair and standing over me in a flash. His hand is on my cheek, the warmth bringing me back to reality.

"Dad? Where am I?" My throat is incredibly dry. "What's going on? Why do I feel like I haven't talked in a week?" It's like I'm discovering the English language for the first time.

"Sweetie, what's the last thing you remember?" I lean back into the bed, and close my eyes. Rubbing my temples, I can think of nothing but my dream. Was it a dream? It had to have been a dream. I feel like I don't know anything anymore.

"Mom..." Dad straightens up and backs into his chair. His knees buckle, and he falls into it so heavily that I'm afraid it might break. He rubs his eyes, and it's then that I can see that he hasn't slept in days. His expression is one of pure exhaustion. "Dad, what's going on?"

He reaches out and takes my hand. "Sweetie, you've been asleep for a week."

My eyebrows furrow as I cock my head to the side. I drag my hand back toward my body and grip the edge of the blanket. I look around, taking in my surroundings for the first time since I woke up. A machine beside me beeps rhythmically, mirroring the beating of my heart. An IV feeds a steady stream of clear liquid into my veins. A tube goes from underneath the blanket to a bag filled with a disgusting yellow fluid. I try to lift my head off the pillow to see beyond the parted curtains, but a doctor blocks my view.

"Ah, Miss Donner, you're awake." My father stands to shake his hand and remains by his side as he approaches the bed. "So nice to see your eyes open, young lady. For a while, I thought your father was lying about how dark they are." He laughs, and my dad tries to join him but finds that his mouth is too dry to make the appropriate sounds. For a second his helpless elf look makes me want to smile, but then I remember the tubes attached to my body and can't seem to lift the corners of my mouth. "You must have a lot of questions." The doctor watches me closely.

I blink slowly, realizing that I hadn't been doing much of that since I opened my eyes. A tear runs down my cheek and slips between my parted lips. I drink it, its descent into my stomach reminding me how thirsty I still am.

"Sleep?" The word barely comes out, and it feels like I just spat dust into the air. My throat is too dry, talking is like blowing off years of dust from an old family album found in the bottom of a box at the back of the attic. I can feel my esophagus contracting like I want to cough, but nothing happens; I just look like I'm choking, which brings the doctor to the head of the bed, my father at his heels.

"Please, don't try to speak. Rest. There will be time for questions later." His hands are on my shoulders as I attempt to keep my head off the pillow. The muscles in my neck give out, and I'm back in the embrace of hospital-grade comfort. I reach for the doctor's arm as he releases my shoulders. He looks down at me, smiles, and squeezes my hand before placing it on the bed. With all of my strength, I push myself up and cough out one word –sleep.

"What?" The doctor looks at my father.

"I told her she has been asleep for a week." The doctor nods and puts his hands on the railing of the bed.

"That's correct, but more accurately, you've been in some sort of a coma. Despite you being unconscious, your brain functioned as if you were awake, which made for a rather interesting coma case, as brain activity tends to be quite low during a coma. Your Deep Limbic System was particularly active. That is where emotional memories are stored." I close my eyes and rub my temples with my middle and pointer fingers.

"When you feel up to it, I would like to know what exactly you were doing before you fell asleep last week." I open my mouth to speak, the idea that anything I did before I went to "sleep" last week could send me into a coma sounds absurd. "Please," he says, holding up his hand, "when you've gotten some rest."

My dad laughs despite himself. "Like she needs more of that." I laugh silently, the humor dissipating the barely stifled tension in the room.

The doctor pats him on the shoulder and laughs with him. "You're right about that, Mr. Donner." I roll my eyes. Did I miss a budding bromance while I was sleeping?

Somehow I'm still able to fall asleep after a week-long nap. When I wake up I can't remember what I dreamt about. Am I even allowed to dream anymore for fear of falling into a coma? I'm sure my dad feels that way, telling by the intense stare he's fixed on me. I can tell by the dark circles under his eyes that he'd been watching me the whole nap. I roll over to my side and stare back.

"Hi." I smile, hoping to break the random tension caused by a nap. "Is there anything I can do for you?" The question comes out more like a croak, my throat even more dry after my nap. My dad rolls his eyes and straightens in the chair.

"You're funny, little girl." He scoots closer to me and hands me a cup of water.

I shift the pillows behind my back and sit up to take a long sip. Drawing my knees to my chest, I continue to stare at my dad. "What's going on?"

My dad stands and takes my hand. "Sweetie, do you think you'll be able to talk to the doctor now? Do you think you're ready to talk about what happened?"

"I don't even know what happened. I didn't know I was asleep till I woke up, if that makes any sense. But yeah, send the doctor in."

He pinches my chin. "Try to reign in the sass, missy." I stick out my tongue and lick his thumb where it lies on my chin. He laughs and wipes his thumb on my hospital gown. "I'll be right back."

I lean into the pillows and close my eyes, knowing sleep won't come for a while after what has been practically a month of unconsciousness. Drawing figure eights in the sheets with my hands, I hum to warm up my vocal chords. I run my thumb down the length of my throat. It feels like I have an itty bitty Adam's apple. I start poking at it, a ridiculous smile spreading across my face as the doctor enters the room.

Sonata

"Miss Donner?" My eyes fly open and my hand falls to my side like a stone in a lake. "Glad to see you've re-acclimated to the waking world." I laugh and nod. "So, are you ready to talk?"

"Yeah. I'm not sure what I'm supposed to tell you." I shrug and take another sip of water.

"How about you just tell me about your day? Tell me what you remember doing before you fell asleep."

I scratch my head. "Which time?"

The doctor laughs. "You're right. Hmm, how about the first time? I don't know how to explain...umm...Mr. Donner?"

"Yes, right, well the last time I saw her awake was the day of the anniversary." My mind immediately goes to that afternoon. Of course that's what I have to talk about. My eyes start to water, so I bring the blanket up to my chin, wanting to hide. "Nita? Are you alright?"

I nod, loosening my grip on the blanket. "Yeah. Well I came home from school and went to my room. My dad left me a snow globe, which I turned on. That's the last thing I remember before falling asleep and waking up to my mother's voice..." I look up at my dad, the color drained from his face. I avert my eyes and focus on the doctor. "I didn't feel like I was in a coma."

"That makes sense. As I mentioned before, your brain was functioning as if you were awake, which is what made this case all the more interesting. From what you have just told me, I can't seem to find any significant triggers that could have caused this. Was anything about the way you fell asleep out-of-the-ordinary or different than normal?"

I rub my eyes. Somehow I'm getting tired again. Is this a symptom of this coma thing? I'm always going to be tired now? I've got to ask the doctor as soon as we figure out the trigger.

"Well, I hadn't seen the snow globe in awhile. My mother gave it to me years ago, then I lost it. As soon as the music started, I felt..." I swallow hard, trying to hold back the tears I let flow freely that night alone in my bedroom. "...like I was drowning in nostalgia. My mind was flooded with memories so overwhelming that all it could do to handle it was shut down. That's when I fell asleep, I guess."

The doctor leans back and taps his chin with his pointer finger. His demeanor says he understands, but none of it makes sense, at least not to me. I don't see the logic in a nostalgia-induced coma, but then again, I'm not a doctor. I can feel my mind filling with ideas to reconcile this whole situation. I'm still slowly getting used to the fact that I'm in a hospital. With a very

Sonata

small smile plastered on my face in an attempt to look calm, I'm sure I look like I'm losing it.

"I'm happy to say that with that, I think I've figured it out." My dad stands level to the doctor and watches as he talks, probably reading his lips instead of actually listening. I find myself doing the same thing, my ears too busy listening to the blood rush to my head to hear a word he's saying. "It seems as though the trauma of losing your mother compounded with the anniversary and the familiar song and object sent you into a deep, "Sleeping Beauty" sleep in which you felt like you were awake. Personally, I think this is how Sleeping Beauty herself felt when she was put under by Maleficent." My dad makes a small huff sound that causes the doctor to laugh. "I mean, I know she's a fictional character, but as a doctor, this is how I look at fairy tales." He looks from my dad to me then back to my dad. Our faces are frozen in concentration and a somewhat stupefied expression. Is this guy really a doctor?

"Okay, forget that, doesn't matter." He waves his hand dismissively. "The point is, your overwhelming sense of nostalgia and sadness caused your body to shut down like when you fall asleep so as to protect your consciousness. It's similar to how you pass out when you're incredibly injured or the fight-or-flight instinct. Sleeping is your body's way of keeping you from feeling severe emotional pain brought on by this snow globe. There's something about the sights and the sounds of the snow globe that inflict an incredible amount of pain on your mind. I don't completely understand that part, but that's more for a psychologist than a neurologist. I'm sure after a while the snow globe will become commonplace in your mind and will no longer knock you out, but I can't say with certainty when that will be. It could be today, it could be a year from now. I advise you to be careful, maybe even return the snow globe to storage."

"No." The word escapes my mouth in a low timbre before I even have time to process what he's saying. It was like it came straight from my heart. Both the doctor and my dad look at me as surprised to hear my voice reach that depth as I am. I clear my throat and sit up straighter in the bed. "I mean, isn't there something I can do?" I look directly into my dad's eyes, trying to connect our souls to impart on him the importance of this memento without actually letting on what it does for me. "I've just missed that snow globe so much..."

My dad crosses in front of the doctor and takes my hand. "Sweetie, I understand, but it's not worth it. This coma condition isn't something to play with."

Sonata

My heart is racing; my palms begin to sweat. I shake off my father's hand and wipe mine on the bed sheets. The doctor puts a hand on our shoulders. He squeezes mine, the heat coming off his fingers reaching through to my thinly clothed skin. "I have to agree with your father. As of right now, we don't have too much information about this type of emotionally charged condition, but I'm hard pressed not to think anything resulting in a coma is good for you. The long term effects could be anywhere from constant fatigue to brain damage. There's really no way to know."

"Then who's to say it's not harmless?" I can barely remember the last time I was as happy as I was in my coma-dreams. Everything felt so real, and there was no pain. It's like the snow globe had answered a prayer I'd been whispering for the past six months. How could I give that up?

"Nita, we're not going to sit here and take up this nice doctor's time having this ridiculous argument. You're going to stop using the snow globe from now on and that's that. Brain damage or no, you can't just check out of life for weeks. You have school and responsibilities." My eyebrows furrow deeply, and I open my mouth to speak, but my father has his finger in my face before I can utter a syllable. "Furthermore, this isn't the life your mother would've wanted for you. Sweetie, you can't just sleep your life away; you have to know that."

He's taken his finger away, and his eyes are welling up. "Dad." I reach out and wrap my fingers around his forearm, my fingers too short to connect. "Okay..."

He puts his hand on top of mine, squeezes gently, then turns to see the doctor out. With their backs turned, I give in to one single tear, allowing it to slide down my face and land between an opening in my gown. The chill of the tear on my bare skin relieves a tiny fraction of the sadness that had been accumulating throughout the whole conversation.

My heart aches in the abyss of my chest, but my eyes are dry. I swing my legs to the side of the bed and let my bare feet touch the cold surface of the hospital floor. Reaching toward the ceiling in a major stretch, I lift my face toward the overhead lights and catch a glimpse of my reflection. I focus on the mirrored surface and run my finger down the length of my cheek, surprised to see my finger reflected on the image that looks more like my mother than me. It's in that moment that I know what I'm going to do – I can't stop seeing her when I close my eyes; I'm just going to have to figure out how to hide it, but how can I hide a week-long nap?

CHAPTER FOUR

Stepping into my bedroom, I'm overcome with a sense of déjà vu for the second time that week. Scratch that – I've been asleep for a week. I guess this would be the second time in two weeks. That doesn't make it sound as bad, I guess. I drop the bag my dad packed for me when he took me to the hospital. I slowly approach my bed and flop face down onto the bouncy mattress. The memory foam topper swallows my groan as I release an animal sound from deep within my throat. My eyelids struggle to meet under the pressure of the mattress, forcing me to look into a darkness that threatens to devour me. I feel like my body is no longer taking up space and nothing is or ever has been real. This whole dream-coma combo has me doubting everything. Is this what tripping on acid feels like?

There's a knock on my door followed by the squeak of its hinges. I roll over onto my back and stare up at my father. "What are you doing?" He asks, an incredulous look on his face.

I blink slowly, my eyes adjusting to sight. Rubbing them raw, I yawn, prolonging my response. My dad waits patiently, knowing full well what I'm doing. The silence calms me and freaks me out simultaneously. I stretch my arms out, my hands grabbing onto my bed frame.

"I'm just being awake, you know, feeling the consciousness around me."

He rolls his eyes. "You're too much these days." I sit up and poke him in the stomach.

"Are you saying you didn't miss me while I was sleeping?" Pushing me over a bit, he sits next to me and puts his arm around my shoulders.

"Sweetie, I was a bit too worried to miss you." I put my head on his shoulder and push my lower lip forward. "But, if I really think about it, I did miss you." We smile at each other and for a minute it's like we've both forgotten everything that makes this weird. "Want to sleep in my bed tonight?" Then another moment goes by, and it all comes back to us.

I pull away from him and lean on my headboard. "Not really." I grab the blanket on my bed and throw it on my nightstand, effectively hiding the snow globe. "Don't you think that would be a bit weird?" He nods

Sonata

and rubs his chin, the faintest five-o'clock-shadow tickling his fingers. "Do you mind giving me a minute alone?"

For a minute, neither of us moves. We stare at each other from different sides of the bed, our eyes mere reflections. I refuse to blink first, the thought that I won't be blinking for a while causing my eyes to well up. He exhales loudly and admits defeat, closing his eyes for longer than a blink. He lifts himself off the bed with his legs, his arms lifeless at his sides. Without looking back, he walks out the door and closes it behind him. I feel bad, but I can't have him around when I hide the snow globe.

I throw the blanket off the nightstand and grab the snow globe by the dome. In my house we have an open door policy, so where could I hide it so that my dad would never find it? I put it under my pillow, but the bulge from the dome makes it too obvious. I stick it under my bed, one of the most obvious hiding places known to man. What is it they say? Hide stuff in plain sight? This counts, right?

Walking backwards toward the door, I try and see if I can spot the snow globe under the bed. I can. From the door, I look around the room to find the best spot, then it hits me. Where would a dad never go, even as a single father of a girl? The underwear drawer of course! I grab the snow globe and rush to my dresser before my dad decides to come back. I dig through to the bottom, burying the snow globe underneath a mound of panties. Nothing says "don't look" like the underwear of the opposite sex; at least that's what I'm hoping.

I hear footsteps coming down the hall, so I jump onto my bed and get under the covers. As expected, my dad opens the door and peeks in. "Time's up." He pushes the door open wide, and strides in coolly. I lift an eyebrow and laugh.

"You're ridiculous." I pat the space beside me. He hops on.

"What'd I miss?" I shove him.

"A phone call from the 80s. They want their swagger back." He tousles my hair. "Hey! I'm not the son you never had." He puts both of his hands over his heart, a grimace on his face.

"Oh, right to the heart!" I laugh and scratch at his shoulder. With my head on his shoulder, he pokes at my nose. "So, have you thought about the sleeping situation?"

I lift my head off his shoulder and lean it against my headboard. "Dad..." His hands appear on my shoulders, leaning me forward.

Sonata

"Sweetie, I'm just worried is all." He looks around the room, his eyes settling on my empty bedside table. "Where's the snow globe?" I look around the room, too, focusing on the side of the room where my dad can't see my face.

"Good question..." I stroke my chin. "Are you sure you didn't move it when we got back from the hospital?" I ask, deflecting blame on him.

He gets up, action in his eyes. Lifting up the blankets on my bed, he pokes around, feeling for the dome. "Where is it?"

I stand on the opposite side of the bed, wanting an unreasonable amount of distance from him and the lie. "Why?"

He stops moving and fixes his gaze on me. "You know why. I can't have you slipping into a coma, young lady." I laugh to lighten the mood and because I don't know what else to do.

"I told you I wasn't going to do it again. Don't you trust me?" My dad puts his middle fingers on his temples and begins to rub.

"Sweetie, you know that's not what this is about..."

"Well, that's what it feels like it's about." Now I'm picking a fight with him. Why am I picking a fight with him?! I'm the one who's lying to his face. I should be kissing his feet right now, but instead I'm throwing acid at them. Alas, there's no going back now.

"The snow globe is obviously not here." I gesture around the room. "So no one will be falling asleep for a week tonight." I fall onto the bed, causing it to bounce ever so slightly, a whimsical movement that detracts from the tension of the current conversation. My dad reaches for my shoulder. I pull away and stare at the opposite wall.

"Sweetie, please don't be mad. I didn't mean to argue, I'm just worried." I rotate my body so I'm facing him while still on the bed. I meet his eyes slowly, making a pit stop at his nose to notice the puddle of undescended snot. I grab his hands and squeeze them reassuringly.

"I know, dad; I just need you to trust me. I don't want you to start handling me with kid gloves from now on. I don't want you to be scared. Please," I say, my voice softening as his eyes move down to stare at the floor, "understand that I'm not going to leave you." He looks up at me, and I focus all of my energy on holding his gaze. "I will always come back."

He kneels on the bed, his legs so long that they're practically still on the floor. His hand hovers in the air between us, shaking.

Sonata

"I'm scared..." I take his hand and hold it on the bed.

"Don't be." He swallows a wad of saliva he had been holding in his mouth. I watch as it moves down his esophagus and makes his Adam's apple dance. He stands and heads toward the door.

"Dad?" He turns around quickly as if he knew I was going to call after him. "I love you." He smiles, the expression falling short of reaching his eyes.

"I love you too, Sweetie. Get some sleep, but not too much." We laugh for a total of two seconds. I point at him from where I'm sitting.

"Good one."

As soon as I hear the creak of my father's door closing, I jump off my bed and run to my door. I open it a crack and peek through, down the hall. With all of the lights turned off, I can't tell if my dad's door is closed, but it doesn't matter at this point. Everyone knows if all the lights are off, it's bedtime.

Taking the hint, I close my door and snatch the snow globe from my underwear drawer. Changing into my pajamas, I can't help but think about how this will affect my relationship with my dad. I just told him I wouldn't do the exact thing that I'm about to do, but how can I not do it? Weighing the thought of upsetting my dad and seeing my mom again, it's a no brainer. Without a second thought, I twist the winding key and put it under my bed. I figure since I'm going to be asleep, I won't be able to hide it before my dad comes in.

    I fluff the pillows and settle under my blanket. Closing my eyes, I can't imagine how I'm going to fall asleep; I'm so excited to see my mom. Although it only feels like a day since I last saw her in my coma-dream, my memories of the pain I felt after she died propels me into dreamland. The snow globe has yet to reach the coda, but I'm already out like the lights in the hallway.

"Mom?" I'm out of my bed before I can remember waking up. "Mom? Where are you?" I take the stairs down two at a time, a serious feat with gravity working against me. As I near the landing, I almost fall on my face. "Mom!"

Sonata

She rounds the corner, and we almost run into each other. "Goodness, lady, what's with all the yelling?"

I grab her shoulders and shake her a bit. Her head bobs back and forth as she laughs. I wrap my arms around her and squeeze as tightly as I can.

"I'm never going to let you go," I whisper in her hair.

"What?" She pulls back from me and stares, a mixture of fright and confusion on her face. "Honey, you're scaring me."

I push her away playfully and laugh it off.

"Calm down, old lady. I'm just playing!" I walk around her, avoiding eye contact. "What's for breakfast?" Walking into the kitchen, I can't fight the feeling of familiarity that creeps up. It's so weird to be in my kitchen but not be in my kitchen at the same time. Somehow, this place feels so different but looks exactly the same.

I pick at the bacon on the table. It's cooked to perfection, the right amount of crisp and chewy fat. The glass of orange juice forms a ring of condensation on the kitchen table. I pick it up and sip loudly, the pulp sticking between my teeth. A shiver runs down my spine as the cold of the juice counteracts the warmth of the day.

"So." Mom slaps her hands on the kitchen table, disturbing the glass that I just put down. "Want to go to the park today?"

"Didn't we go to the park the other day?" I move to the stove where a frying pan full of scrambled eggs sits cooling.

"What are you talking about?" She joins me and hands me a fork from the drawer. "We haven't gone to the park in weeks. You've been too busy with school and finishing the semester, remember?" She's wearing a duh look on her face as she munches.

It occurs to me that my dream-coma may not be linear. Waking up could disrupt the flow of this world, just as falling asleep messes with the other one. This whole situation is going to keep me confused, I just know it, but it's worth it. Even if I wake up and my dad has found and destroyed the snow globe, it would all have been worth it for this one moment with my mom.

That's really all I've wanted; knowing that this could be the last, I feel the moment creating an etching in my brain. Is it possible that it's this easy? Does knowing the exact limit of our time together make the idea of losing one another that less painful? I sure hope so, because I can't imagine I can keep sneaking back to this world.

Sonata

I give myself a light tap on the head with my fist. "You're so right! Yeah, let's go to the park!" Mom drops her fork and turns to grab the picnic blanket from the living room. I watch her as she exits the kitchen and listen as she hums under her breath. I drum on the kitchen counter, my beat fattening her melody.

"Hop to it, chicken legs." She's out the door and on the sidewalk before I can even grab my keys. We run toward the park, arm-in-arm, the breeze chasing after us, pushing us forward. I breathlessly race through the gates and extend my arms.

"Victory!" My mom is close behind me, pushing me to take my place just inside the gate.

"Good job. You beat an old lady at a race. Do you feel good about yourself?" I stroke my chin and gaze into the sky, my eyes darting back and forth as if that were a real question to consider.

"Yeah, yeah I do," I say, looking back at her with a smug grin on my face.

The park is exactly as I remember it from last time. The leaves are dancing in the sky to music only they can hear, and children are chasing each other around the jungle gym, their laughter floating above our heads. It feels like the day is going to repeat itself, like in this world there is only one day - only one day that

I get to be with my mom and live in over and over again. If that's a side effect of this coma-dream, I'd be okay with that. I watch as my mom jumps to disturb the leaves in their flight pattern, and I know I'd be okay with that.

I walk past her toward the trail that weaves in and out of the dense forest at the center of the park, hoping she will follow me. She does, slipping her arm into the crook of mine. Hugging my arm, she leans her head on my shoulder, a position that makes walking difficult for the both of us, but neither of us minds right now. Our pace slows, and we walk in silence with only the sounds of the birds in the nearby trees as a soundtrack. I inhale deeply, the mixture of her perfume and the musk of the forest creating an intoxicating scent that I'm sure if I smelled it anywhere else would bring me back to this moment. With my free arm outstretched, I can just barely reach the trees, my fingertips grazing the bark as we pass by.

In any other world, I would be bored. This whole scene, a moment between a mother and a daughter, looks so cliché from the outside. Nothing matters but us two, and it seems fake, like a dream world I wouldn't usually be dreaming about. As we move at a glacial pace, I wonder what's going to break this strange moment we seem paralyzed in. The sounds of

Sonata

the birds in the trees become bothersome as they drown out my own thoughts and the sound of my mother's breathing. My tongue is lying dead on the floor of my mouth, saliva congealing on its surface. I'm all too aware of every inch of my body as I half drag myself onward, the weight of my mother's head on my shoulder almost too much to take on at this pace. I stop and the moment stops with me.

"Is everything alright, honey?" My shoulder feels like it could float off into space as soon as she lifts her head. I sigh, wondering how I can make this world feel normal. "Hello?" She's waving her hand in front of my face, my eyes glazed over in thought. "Is there anybody home up there?"

I blink slowly, feeling as my eyelids connect and sweep over my eyeballs. Sighing again, I stretch both of my arms upward and lean to the side, hitting my mom with my extended arms. "I think I just fell asleep for a second there." My mom's eyebrows furrow. "Could this walk be any more boring?" Her face breaks into a grin, and she starts to poke me. "Hey now," I say as she continues to poke me.

"You're it!" She takes off down the path without even a glance back at my motionless form. I stare after her as my body recognizes the challenge. With a quick shake of each leg, I'm running after her. Just as I'm catching up to her, she jumps off the path and into the forest, the trees hiding her as soon as she enters. Without hesitation, I follow her, knowing the forest like the back of my hand from childhood years playing hide-and- seek with Jordan. As I run through the forest, dodging branches and unearthed roots, I can't help but think – now this is more like it.

"Mom, won't you stay up with me?" I pat the space beside me, inviting her to join me on my bed for yet another movie.

"Honey, I think I'm all rom-commed out for the night." She laughs and adjusts the pillows so that I'm forced to sink into a lying position. "We both need rest after today."

"Who knew you had so much pep in your step, old lady. For a second, I thought I was going to lose."

She picks up a pillow and throws it at my head. Catching it, I stick out my tongue and situate it behind me. "I let you win."

"That's what a sore loser would say."

"Whatever." She rolls her eyes and sits on the edge of the bed. "Whatever helps you sleep at night, honey."

Sonata

I stare into her eyes, taking mental photos of every half movement of her eyebrows, every twitch of her nose, and every wrinkle around her mouth. Despite my fatigue, I can't even think of sleeping. Maybe it's because I know somewhere in another world I'm already sleeping. My body is completely awake, and by the look on my mom's face, she knows that. I try to flutter my eyes as if I'm drifting off, but my eyelids stubbornly remain open, my eyes unwilling to tear themselves away from my mom for fear that she might disappear if they do.

"I know what will knock you out." She twists her body to face my bedside table. Sitting there amongst a frenzy of notecards and pencils is my snow globe. She shakes it, causing the artificial flakes to cascade down on the immobile ice skaters.

I hold my hand out and put it over hers. "Please don't." My arm feels heavy as the first chord of Beethoven's Piano Sonata fills the room. Mom stands and smooths her nightgown. She walks to the door, taking a second to turn back to me and blow me a kiss.

"I love you, honey." My arm is still outstretched, but it lies on my bed where my mom once sat.

"Mom..." I can't even get the words out of my mouth before I fall asleep. That is one damn good lullaby, Beethoven.

CHAPTER FIVE

I know where I am before I even open my eyes. I can smell the sterile air of the hospital, and I'm scared that my dad won't be in the room waiting for me to wake up like the last time. I try to continue breathing as if I'm still asleep. Opening my eyes slightly, I can see the top of my dad's shoes, dull with neglect. I lift my eyes to meet his, which are open and watching me. He's frowning and isn't even phased when I look at him, his expression blank as a sheet of paper. I push myself up into a sitting position and bring my knees up to my chest. With my hands on top of my knees, I lay my head down and take a deep breath, holding it until the silence is broken.

"You know what I'm going to say." I close my eyes and nod against my knees.

Sonata

"I'm sorry." When I open my eyes, tears run down my cheeks and into my mouth. I swallow, focusing on the burn of the saltwater as it slides down my esophagus. My dad scoots his chair closer and slides one of my hands out from under my chin. He closes his fingers around my own and squeezes.

"Sweetie, I know you are. I don't want you to think I'm mad. I'm not mad, Sweetie, I'm worried. You know there are probably medical implications to this." With that, it's like his face melts. His eyes are shiny with unshed tears, and his mouth forms a wavy line that's neither a frown nor a smile.

I turn my hand over in his and squeeze back. "I know! I just miss her so much..."

He sits on the bed and puts his arm around my shoulders. "Me too, Sweetie, me too." I lean my head on his shoulder and close my eyes.

"You just don't understand. When I'm asleep, I see her. In this dream-coma I can feel her, talk to her, do things with her." I look up at him earnestly from my position on his shoulder.

His chin hits the top of my head as he tries to make eye contact. He pushes me back so that he can really see my face. I avert my eyes. I didn't know what I was thinking - that he would believe me? Tears stream down my face as I imagine his condescending remarks about how I'm probably seeing things and how these unconscious spells are messing with my mind. Right now, I don't think I can deal with any doubt that these moments with my mom aren't real.

"Can we go home now?" All I want is to be in my bed. The sterility of the hospital breaks my heart. It's so impersonal, and I'm longing for the rows of family photos that line the living room. I throw the rough blanket off and gather the gown behind me to cover my butt. My dad hesitates for a minute then tosses a duffle bag onto the bed.

I take out the jeans and t-shirt he packed for me. "We have to wait for the doctor, but you can go ahead and put your clothes on. I'll be outside the curtain, Sweetie." He reaches over and squeezes my wrist then leaves.

I slide the jeans on underneath my gown. For some reason I'm exhausted, so much so that I have to lean on the bed and take a break before putting on my shirt. My breath comes in rough and shallow, and I'm beginning to feel light headed.

I'm scared to admit it, but I know what this is. I mean, I don't know what it is exactly - I'm not a doctor - but I know why I feel this way. I know I'm not being smart, but I have to hide this struggle to breathe. I close my eyes and inhale through my nose as deeply as my body will allow. I blow the air out through my mouth. My cheeks expand as the air collects and it's as if I'm blowing out the candles on a birthday cake. I lie back on the bed and wait for the doctor to come in. I don't move when I hear the whoosh of the curtains being pulled back and the sound of two pairs of footsteps.

"Ok, Miss Donner, your tests look good. You're exhibiting a slight increase in blood pressure, but it's nothing to be concerned about for now. I am getting a bit concerned about these visits, though. Tell me, did you use the snow globe again?" The doctor is looming over me, thankfully blocking the fluorescent light.

What am I supposed to tell him? The truth is not an option. Like a doctor would believe my snow globe story. Sometimes I don't even believe it. Could there be any scientific reason I'm having these - these what? Delusions? Dreams? Could the doctor figure it out if I tell him what's been happening? I look at my dad and can tell we're on the same page. We don't need to be known as the Delusional Donners at this hospital, and I have a feeling we're going to be coming back again and again and again.

"I really don't know what to tell you, doc. I'm not doing anything else special before I pass out."

Rishire Young

"Are you sure there's nothing small you might have done both times that you don't usually do? I'm finding it hard to believe a snowglobe can cause a coma once, nonetheless twice."

I tap my chin as if I'm deep in thought - maybe just shallow in thought. I let out a soft hmm to let the doctor know I'm really searching the archives for these memories. "I'm coming up blank. Nothing comes to mind."

The doctor leans back and puts his hands in the pockets of his white coat. He doesn't look happy, and I'm afraid he's going to keep pushing me. Instead he says, "Look, Miss Donner, I know you're not telling me everything. I don't know why you're keeping something from me, but I'm sure you have your reasons. I just hope you and your father understand how serious this could be. Medically speaking, you're not exhibiting anything overtly concerning, which leads me to believe that these comas aren't an actual threat to your health. However, these week-long periods of unconsciousness will cause your breathing to be labored once in a while, akin to asthma, but that won't greatly affect your respiratory system. That being said, this is not a way to live, Miss Donner. Whatever reasons you have for nodding off like this -whether it be because you think it may be the ultimate beauty sleep or

Sonata

school is too stressful right now - they don't amount to how amazing life can be when you take the chance to live it."

My dad is nodding his head fervently in agreement, boring holes into the doctor's head with his eyes as if trying to communicate telepathically. The doctor looks at him and shakes his head slightly. I've heard all I need to hear. These comas won't kill me, so there's no reason for me not to keep using the snowglobe and seeing my mom. I stare at the ceiling and let the lights screw with my vision. Colorful dots pop into sight every time I blink, and it's a nice distraction from what feels like a lecture on how to live.

"You're free to go. I really hope you take what I said to heart and monitor your activities. I don't want to see you back here again any time soon, Miss Donner."

I nod. Is there a way to request a different doctor, because I have a feeling I will be back in this hospital very soon. I scoot off the bed and grab the duffel bag. My dad follows the doctor out and shakes his hand before he turns to go. I reach out to touch his arm but withdraw my hand at the last second. I have a feeling my dad isn't too happy with me, and that feeling is confirmed when he walks off toward the exit without a glance back at me. I swallow the lump that has been forming in my throat and follow him to the car.

Rishire Young

The ride home is completely silent. I don't even try to make conversation; I don't know what I would say. The radio isn't on, and I don't want to be the one who turns it on. I don't want to move at all. My hands remain in my lap, my fingers intertwined and palms touching as if in prayer. Maybe I should pray; I haven't in awhile. Before I can even think up an opening statement, we're home and my dad is out of the car in a flash.

I sit in the car not knowing what to do with myself. I don't even know what day it is. I reach back for the duffel bag and dig out my phone. As it powers on, I try to come up with a game plan. I'm not sure if I should talk to my dad about this, but I refuse to stop - I refuse to give up the one link to my mother that actually allows me to touch her, talk to her, spend time with her. I can make new memories with her, and to me that's more important than whatever "amazingness" life has to offer. Just the thought of never going back to that world, of going back to before I got the snow globe, to the soul-crushing sadness that makes me feel like a black hole has formed in my heart, sucking in all of my emotions and leaving me with nothing but numbness, makes my whole body ache. My dad can't want that for me. More importantly, I don't want that for me.

Sonata

Without waiting for my phone to completely power on, I throw the car door open and run into the house. I forgot to worry about my dad being alone in the house where my room and the snow globe are. I drop the duffel bag by the door and take the stairs two at a time. My bedroom door is open, and my breath catches in my throat as I approach cautiously. Stopping beside the doorway, I swallow hard and inhale deeply, holding my breath in the hollow of my chest. I step into the room and exhale with a whoosh as I see that it's empty and the snow globe is safe on my bedside table.

My dad has been in here, though. I can tell because I remember hiding the snow globe underneath my bed before I went to sleep that night a week ago. I walk over to my bedside table and put my palm on the dome of the snow globe. The glass is cool, and my fingers stick to it. I sit on my bed and take the snow globe by the base, placing it in my lap. I don't twist the winding key. It's too soon; I just got back. I wonder why my dad didn't destroy it when he had the chance. He had a whole week to break it or hide it, and yet he put it on my bedside table as if giving me permission to use it. Is that what he's doing? Giving me permission to use it?

Rishire Young

There's a clatter of pots and pans in the kitchen. I go downstairs and find my dad there, cooking what looks like a dinner for two. He can't be too mad at me if he's making me dinner, right?

"Are you going to just stand there or are you going to help me make dinner?"

It's like he snaps his fingers, I am at his side so fast. "What do you want me to do?"

He hands me a pot full of vegetables without speaking, and I hang my head and turn on the faucet, filling the pot with hot water. I listen to the clicking of the stove as the fire flares up. The blue flames lick at the stovetop, and the heat wafts up to caress my cheek. Faint, white smoke creeps up the pot as soon as I put it on the stove.

I can still feel the heat as it travels through the pot, to the water, then to the vegetables. Within minutes, the water bubbles and some of the vegetables rise to the top. I turn the dial, lowering the fire, then turn to lean on the counter beside the stove. My dad moves around the kitchen like a snake in the grass except less sinister. I'm not sure that is the best comparison, but his movements are so fluid it's like he and the kitchen are one, and they have no bones. He's smiling despite himself, his love of cooking overtaking his anger toward me. He catches me staring and a slight frown

Sonata

replaces the smile. I look away, turning toward the pot as if I'm actively willing the vegetables to cook. The silence is killing me. It's so quiet I think I can hear the flapping of a fly's wings. I clear my throat, making a guttural sound that echoes through the kitchen.

"The vegetables are coming along nicely..." I can't even look at my dad. My small talk needs some work.

"What?" Good. He didn't hear what I said. Now's my chance to say something more substantial but uncomplicated. What to say; what to say...

"Do you have work tomorrow? I was thinking we could go to the zoo then do dinner and a movie."

He's right by my ear when he says, "Sure, Sweetie." I jump, my hand going down on the handle of the pot, not enough to flip it off the stove, but enough to spill some water onto my bare, left foot. My mouth can't keep up with my mind. I think about yelping before I can open my mouth. My dad takes my arm and guides me to a barstool. He takes my hand, and I squeeze it like a woman in labor.

"Dad, dad, dad." The words come out as exhalations. My foot is throbbing and turning the slightest shade of red, the only shade it can muster. Tears are streaming down my face, and my mouth is opening and closing like a fish's.

Rishire Young

My dad releases my hand and reaches for his phone. "I'll call the emergency room, let them know we're on our way." I put my hand over his.

"No. You heard what the doctor said this morning or whatever time of day it was. I don't need to become a regular at the hospital. It's not a Starbucks."

"Forget what the doctor said. You can go to the hospital as many times as you need to." He closes his fingers around his cellphone and pushes my hand off of his.

"Dad, it's not that big of a deal. I just need to soak my foot in some lukewarm water, nothing too cold; I think that could damage the nerves or something due to the sudden change in temperatures." I stand, supporting myself with my right leg, and hop-skip to the sink. "Could you get me a deep pan or a large bowl, something my feet can fit in."

I can hear my dad hesitating, feel him looking from me to his cell phone and back again. I turn on the faucet, running the cold water over my hand to check the temperature. As the water gets colder, my dad searches through the cabinets for a pan or a bowl. He places a long, plastic bowl into the sink, a bowl that looks perfect for soaking feet.

The water rises in the bowl, making waves as the stream lands. I look up at my dad then back to the

Sonata

bowl. He shrugs and murmurs so low I can barely hear him. "It was your mom's." His shoulders are still by his ears in a paused shrug. I nod while still watching the water fill the bowl.

The bowl is heavy when I lift it out of the sink. My dad takes it from me and walks over to the living room, putting it on the floor in front of the couch. I begin limping toward him until he takes my arm over his shoulders and practically carries me to the couch. I slide my feet into the bowl one toe at a time, testing the temperature. I involuntarily sigh when my left foot is submerged.

I still don't know what time it is, but I'm beginning to get sleepy. I yawn as my dad hands me a plate of food. "You were right. The vegetables came out nicely." I laugh, a forkful of carrots, broccoli, and asparagus halfway to my mouth. He sits next to me, his own plate of food resting precariously on his lap. He grabs the remote and switches on Animal Planet. I roll my eyes but settle in for an hour of Dirty Jobs.

Dishes are piled up in the sink, and my dad is lightly snoring on the couch. My foot is feeling better, so I walk up the stairs, trying not to wake my dad up with the creak of every step. I slide into my room and put on my pajamas. I'm exhausted, so I dive onto my bed above my comforter. As soon as my head hits the pillow, my mind drifts off, but not toward a dream, toward nothing, and I couldn't be happier. The darkness that envelops me is comforting. I'm so tired of having so many thoughts, of thinking of my mom and how much I miss her and how much I can't live without seeing her everyday.

Before I can completely fall asleep, a soft knock on the door takes my attention. "Sweetie?" My dad comes in and kneels by my bed. I lay on my side and curl up, making myself small, Daddy's little girl. He smiles down at me and looks at the snow globe. "I know you've noticed I left the snow globe out in the open. I didn't want to go to bed without explaining - I trust you. I understand why you keep doing this, I really do, but you can't blame me for wanting you to stop."

"Dad..." He holds up his hand.

"Let me finish. I want you to stop, but I know you won't. The thing is...you can't keep missing school. Your grades are dropping, and as unimportant as that may seem in the grand scheme of things, I know you'll feel better if you finish. So I have a bit of a compromise for you - if you promise to not use the snow globe for the rest of the school year and go to class, bring up your grades, I'll support whatever decision you make for the summer. If you want to spend the whole summer in this other world and in a coma, I'll do whatever needs to be done to keep you healthy and safe while you're sleeping."

I swallow hard, the saliva in my mouth like a medicine I don't want to take but know will make me feel better. It makes sense now, the snow globe on my bedside table, the permission he nonverbally gave. I really don't know what to think of this compromise. It sounds good, but can I really hold off on seeing my mom for two months? My dad's eyes fill with tears, and it stabs at my heart. I grab his hands and squeeze as hard as I can.

"Daddy, thank you. I know how hard this must've been for you, giving me permission to check out for the whole summer. I miss her, and I love you so much for this. Don't worry; I won't use the snow globe again until school ends."

My dad closes his eyes, causing the tears to stream down his face. He nods and squeezes my hands as he stands. Reaching down and stroking my hair, he whispers, "I love you so much, Nita. I love you so much."

I hate seeing my dad this way, but I just can't give up my mom. I already lost her once; I'm not doing it again. If only he could come to the dream-coma with me and see for himself what it's like. I'm sure he wouldn't want to stop either, real life be damned. We could be a family again, and things could go back to the way they were. I love both of my parents so much, and it's hard leaving one for the other, but I think that this grief has changed the way that I love them.

I see my dad every day in a way that's normal and acceptable, but these moments with my mom are few and far between. They're otherworldly, so I have to grab them when I can before I can't anymore. My dad is sad about it now, but I'm sure he'll get over it, because the fact is, I'll still be here in the real world more often then I'll be in the dream-coma, so nothing is really lost. Since I still get to spend time with my mom, that couldn't be more true.

CHAPTER SIX

The sun is attempting to pry my eyes open. I groan and lay face down on my pillow. It can't possibly be time to get up yet. I feel like I've been sleeping for a second. The conversation with my dad played over and over in my head all of last night, and I couldn't stop thinking of how selfish I'm being. I can see that it's hurting him, me being in a coma. I lean over to the side and inhale deeply. The air catches in my chest and I sit up, coughing and spluttering like water had just gone down the wrong pipe.

I tiptoe downstairs and grab a glass from the cupboard. I hold my hand under running water and feel as it turns from room temperature to cold. I fill the cup and keep the water running as I sip. As soon as I empty the cup, I fill it back up, again and again, so much that I don't even know how many glasses of water I've had.

Rishire Young

My eye catches the calendar on the far wall of the kitchen, and I sigh. It's Sunday. That means school is in less than 24 hours. These little coma vacations have made me forget what it's like to have a schedule. I'm definitely not looking forward to going back to that, to a place where people will ask me prying questions, stare at me, wonder where I've been for the last couple of weeks.

I rub my eyes, feeling how squishy my eyeballs are, almost wishing I could pop them. It's then that I make a decision to sleep for the rest of the day. I can only imagine how tired I'm going to be at school tomorrow without my seven-day nap.

School is just as bad, no worse, than I thought it would be. My dad must've served up some sob story to cover my disappearance. He may have even mentioned my hospitalizations and showed them a few doctor's notes - that would really clinch it. Whatever he told the principal got me a full day pass to spend some quality time with one of my favorite people at the school - Mrs. Miskole. Luckily I've already come up with a game plan in the event that I'm extensively questioned.

Sonata

Step one: Be incredibly vague. Whether or not they know about my hospitalizations, my mentioning it can't be suspicious in any way. Who wants to dig deep into a girl's hospitalization? It's personal stuff, and I'll make it clear that's how I feel about it.

Step two: Cry a little. Make a big show of trying to hold back tears. Breathe in an unusual pattern that could go to explaining my time in the hospital. A fit of hyperventilation would even pause the interrogation, a total win-win.

Step three: Talk in circles. I'm basically doing that right now. I didn't actually do much planning, this is really on-the-fly type stuff.

As usual, Mrs. Miskole is waiting for me outside her office door. Her smile is forced and full of a sadness I'm not used to seeing on her face. I falter a bit as I walk toward her, unsure now about lying to her. I give her my warmest smile, which, to be honest, is maybe a degree or two warmer than room temperature. I consider hugging her but think better of it, knowing that the random and uncharacteristic show of affection would be suspicious. Instead I slide past her into her office and take a seat in my usual chair beside the couch. She nods as if agreeing with a statement she thought to herself while she closes the door.

"It's good to have you back, Miss Donner." I widen my smile and hold my hands in my lap.

"It's good to be back, Mrs. Miskole." Part of me thinks I actually mean it. Mrs. Miskole's smile becomes more genuine, making me think she can tell I almost mean it, too.

"That's really good to hear. Could you tell me what's been going on with you?"

"Nothing of note really." Be vague. I repeat, be vague. "It's just been really hard since my mom passed away, as you know." My throat aches with the tears I don't want to cry, and the nonchalance hurts my heart. My pause doesn't go unnoticed.

"Let's talk about that. The last time I saw you, the last time any of us saw you, was the six month anniversary of the accident. I can't help but think that's not a coincidence."

I nod, my eyes filling with tears as per step two. I would like to say I'm effectively playing Mrs. Miskole, but honestly this is getting to me. This whole time I haven't really had to think about losing my mom, because it was like she was still with me. Knowing I can't see her again like I have been is making this more real than it's been for a couple of weeks.

"I don't know what to say."

Sonata

Mrs. Miskole nods. "You know, sometimes not saying anything is more therapeutic. Just let yourself feel. Release your inhibitions and don't hold back. This is a safe space, and we can take as long as you want. Just let me know when you want to open up a dialogue."

I lean back in my chair and let my head hit the back of it. My eyes leak into my ears, filling them like little pools. I close them and let my breathing slow. My heart starts to beat faster as my mind wanders, a collage of moments with and memories of my mom fill my mind's eye. I can't stop myself; I'm too deep in my mind. I'm feeling too much, and my body can't hold it all in. I start to shake as the sobs tear through my body. I keep my eyes closed, so I can pretend I'm alone, pretend that Mrs. Miskole isn't sitting a few feet away, watching me with clinical eyes.

The chair is becoming uncomfortable as the sadness weighs me down. I wish I had chosen the couch like she always suggests. My limbs are too heavy to move, and I feel like I'm gradually sinking into the floor, soon to go through it and end up in the basement. The silence becomes less therapeutic, but there's nothing that seems worth saying. I can feel Mrs. Miskole getting restless, the silence feeling like the antithesis of therapy. She said I could take all the time I want, and I want this whole day to pass in a silence that isn't so much comforting as it is less bothersome than talking. I guess Mrs. Miskole was right - silence can be therapeutic.

The rest of the week flies by as clichéd as that sounds. It goes by in a blink of an eye, and before I know what happens it's the weekend again, and I couldn't be happier. The sight of my bedroom gives me pause, though. There is a stack of assignments as tall as me on my desk, and I've got a feeling I have until Monday to finish it all. The teachers were all very nice to me on my first day back, but after a while, you could tell they expect me to catch up ASAP. Good thing I've always been known to be an average student. No need to start knocking it out of the park now.

It's been such a long time since I've sat at my desk that my butt has forgotten how the chair feels. I scoot as close to my desk as I can get and pull out the first book. I'm staring at the pages, and nothing makes sense. The words blur in front of me, and I can't understand any of it. I open my eyes as wide as I can and really focus on the page. It's a math textbook - algebra - which explains why the words didn't make sense. Who thought it was a good idea to put letters in math problems? In what world do letters show up in a real world calculation?

Sonata

I close the book and lie my head on the cover. Maybe if I take a short nap this will start to make sense. If I just close my eyes and let myself think of something else, I'll nail this math. I'll just take a twenty minute nap - a power nap!

The next thing I know, it's dark outside and the clock reads 7:30 pm. I lift my head, blinking rapidly and wiping drool off my chin. Reaching out toward the ceiling, I let out a loud yawn and crack my neck. I push away from the desk and roll to my bed where I basically slide underneath the covers. Nowadays it's like I spend all of my time on my back.

Snuggling deeper into the mattress, I can't imagine getting up again, going to school again, dealing with life again. My eyes sweep over the snow globe on my bedside table, and it's like a fist has formed around my heart, squeezing in some phantom way that hurts on another level. I squeeze my eyes shut and throw the covers over my head, the world going darker, the air getting thicker, and the day ending in stillness.

I can feel the days passing over me, the months that separate me from my mom. I go to school, I come home, I do everything in a fog, a haze on which I float. Somehow I don't fail and I'm able to finish my sophomore year with passable grades. Sure, I won't be in any AP classes my junior year, but I can't get myself to care, I can't get myself to think beyond the memories I plan to make with my mom, the memories I know won't be real no matter how real they feel.

As fast as the last few months have gone by, these last few minutes are ticking away like hours. I sit in the back row of English class, watching the hands on the clock move at a glacial pace. Mrs. Haim's voice drones on in the background, sounding like a teacher's in a Charlie Brown movie. The school year is basically done, so I don't even bother paying attention until I hear my name.

"Nita?" I shift my focus from the clock to the boy sitting in front of me, his back twisted so he's facing me while still sitting at his desk. "You're Nita Beth Donner, right?" I nod slowly. "Well, Mrs. Haim just assigned us to be partners for this summer's pen pal project."

Since when does a high school have a pen pal project? It seems a bit elementary school-ish, but I smile and nod anyway. "Oh yeah. I totally just heard her say that. Not sure what I'll have to pen about this summer, but I guess I can send you a few letters." The boy whose name I don't know but should definitely figure out before class ends laughs as if he knows I haven't heard a word anyone's said since I woke up this morning.

Sonata

"I know what you mean. I don't have any real plans this summer. How about we just hang out instead? I mean, I'm not going anywhere, and from what you just said, you're staying in town too. We're actually neighbors; not sure if you knew that!" I smile as if I totally knew that. Awkward...He smiles back and reaches out his hand. "My name is Gabriel, by the way. Most people call me Gabe."

I shake his hand, my head bobbing up and down with every shake. For a second I forget I actually have summer plans - plans that don't involve me getting out of bed nonetheless going next door to hang out. This kid, Gabe, won't understand something like that, so I open my mouth to lie to him about some sort of summer camp or major grounding when the bell rings. I look at the clock and find that the five minutes I had been counting down flew by as we talked. I guess a watched clock doesn't tick. Figures.

"I'll see you around Nita Beth!" And with that, he's gone, out the door and possibly to my house since we're neighbors and apparently best friends now.

"It's just Nita..." I call after him half-heartedly.

CHAPTER SEVEN

As soon as I get in the house I slide my book bag off and leave it by the front door. The day has been wearing on me since I woke up this morning, and all I want to do is go back to bed, maybe for a whole week. Before I can drag myself to the stairs, the sound of my dad's laughter coming from the living room catches my attention. What are the chances this Gabe guy beat me to my own house?

I turn the corner and find my dad lounging on the couch beside Jordan. I stop dead in my tracks, the surprise evident on my all too worn out face. They carry on as if they didn't notice my entrance, which they very well might not have. I lean on the door frame and clear my throat theatrically.

"Honey, there you are! It's about time you got home! How did Jordan beat you here?"

Jordan and my dad smile up at me, and it takes every muscle in my face to smile back. "I guess she

Sonata

knows some back roads that I don't. You're going to have to teach me those sometime."

Jordan laughs like I've told the world's funniest joke. "Nita, I'm pretty sure I saw you napping by your locker after the last bell. Didn't you get any sleep last night, or were you just so excited about the end of the year party at my house?"

Oh, that. "Oh, that. I don't think I can go this year. I have so much stuff to do around the house, right Dad?" I try to make eye contact with my dad, try to communicate with him telepathically, but of course he's avoiding my gaze.

"No! Your dad seemed pretty excited that you're coming. You are coming right? You have the whole summer to do stuff around the house, right Mr. Donner?"

I watch in horror as my dad smiles at Jordan and nods. "But Dad, I'm going away for the summer, remember?!" Why is he doing this? Is this his way of going back on his promise? Did he destroy the snow globe while I was at school?!

He finally turns to me, revealing a sadness in his eyes that I'm sure Jordan hasn't noticed. "No, honey, I didn't forget." His eyes fill with tears. He blinks rapidly, forcing the tears back into their ducts, a trick I know all too well. "You've got some time, though. Go to the party. Hang out with your friends for a week or two before you go. I can tidy up around here by myself. Go have fun. Please..."

The last word is only loud enough for me to hear. My eyes sting, so I close them before they can flood. I nod slowly and turn to leave. "I'll go get ready."

Jordan lets out a high pitched squeal and jumps off the couch. "I'll see you in a few hours!" She hurries out the door, closing it behind her like she lives here.

I stop in the foyer and wait for my dad to join me. He slides his arm around my shoulders and presses his cheek to mine. "I love you, Honey. Don't be mad."

My shoulders sag, and I lean my head into his. "I'm not mad, Dad. I love you too..."

I'm zipping up my skirt when the doorbell rings. "Dad, can you get that please! It's probably just Jordan picking me up for the party," I yell out my door. I don't know why she always insists we walk over to her house together; she lives five blocks away. I hear my dad's heavy footsteps rumble down the stairs. The front door creaks as he opens it, and I hear a slightly familiar voice greet my dad.

Sonata

"Sweetie, it's your friend, Gabe!" Gabe?! What's he doing here? I slip on my black sandals, grab my little, black crossbody bag, and bound down the stairs.

"Hey..." Gabe is standing inside the doorway, the door still open behind him, his hands clasped in front of him, looking like the perfect gentleman. "What are you doing here?"

He steps toward me, and it takes every muscle in my body to keep myself from stepping back. "I ran into Jordan outside a few hours ago, and she insisted I go to her end of the year party. I figured since we're pen pals and she said you're going, I would go too and walk with you to her house."

"Interesting. I've never seen you at one of Jordan's parties."

"Yeah, I don't usually go. The last day of school is usually when I take a break from the school social scene." I raise my eyebrows and smirk.

"Oh, I didn't know you were so popular." Gabe shrugs, the tiniest movement of his shoulders. I look at my phone and sigh. "I guess we should get going. I wanted to go early so I could leave early."

He bends his elbow, offering it to me as a gentleman would. I ignore him, walking past him and down the street. "Ok then." He follows me, skipping ahead a bit so he can walk backwards and look at me. "Do you have a hot date tonight? Is that why you want to leave early."

Heat rises to my face, and I look down at my shoes. "No, I'm just a little tired." He continues to skip backwards flawlessly. As I watch him skip, I notice how cute he is. His eyes are the darkest eyes I've ever seen, his lips are full, and he has a little button nose that couldn't be cuter. He stops skipping and falls into step with me. I inhale deeply, his scent, a mixture of freshly chopped wood and Irish Spring body wash, fills my nose. I smile despite myself and wonder how I'd never noticed him before.

"I noticed. You were beyond out of it in English class."

"Oh, you noticed that? I thought I hid it well." He laughs and pushes me lightly. I can still feel the warmth of his hand as if it were still on my arm. A tingling sensation runs through my body. I shake out my arm, and the warmth is gone. "So..."

"Hey, Gabe!" Chris Gleeson runs up to us and claps Gabe on the back. "Wasn't expecting to see you out and about on the last day of school."

Gabe motions to me. "I got some incentive this year. You know Nita, right?"

I nod to Chris. I know Chris just about as much as I know anyone else in my grade. He's on the basketball team, which means we don't run in the same circles. My circle is more like a dot really.

Chris nods in my direction and returns his attention to Gabe. "This is sick! You've got to get on wingman duty tonight, man. Janice is gonna be there."

Gabe pats him on the back and smiles. "I got you, man." Chris bounces up and down and runs up Jordan's driveway.

I laugh. "Mr. Popular," I say under my breath. He nudges me.

"Hey, I heard that." I bite my lip to keep from giggling.

Music is pouring out of Jordan's house. The door is wide open, and I can see people drinking from solo cups and lounging on the sofa. I make my way to the food table and grab a handful of pretzels. Gabe is still by my side, looking around as if he'd just entered an alternate universe.

"Jordan throws this party every year?" He's still looking around, his mouth slightly open in surprise.

"Yeah," I shout over the music. "It doesn't seem like a Jordan thing to do, but ever since her older sister graduated, she's taken it upon herself to keep the tradition going. She even tries to join in on the fun, but most of the time we hang out in her room and make up stories about what's going on down here."

Gabe looks at me with raised eyebrows. "You don't like to party either?"

I shrug. "I don't know. I never really had the chance being friends with Jordan. This is the only party we go to, the only party we're invited to."

I never thought about it, but it's kind of sad. Spending the whole party in Jordan's bedroom talking - is that really what I like doing? I like this music, and I've always imagined the typical high school party, but I just stick with Jordan. I always stick with Jordan, because she's my best and only friend. That's never been a problem before, so why am I questioning it now?

"Nita!" Jordan is speeding down the stairs toward us. "I'm so glad you made it! And you brought Gabe!"

"Hey, Jordan. Thanks for the personal invite." Gabe grins at Jordan, his dimples creating craters in his cheeks. "Killer turnout. If I had known your parties were like this, I would've been coming to them." Jordan blushes, her whole face, even her ears, turning red. I cover my mouth to stifle a laugh.

"So, Nita, wanna come upstairs?" She's already backing away, confident that I'm going to follow her.

"You know what, I think I'm gonna stay down here, hang out with my new friend, Gabe. You should stay too! Enjoy the party you're throwing!"

Sonata

I'm putting on Jordan-esque enthusiasm. Jordan kicks at the floor. She clears her throat and scratches her head. I can see the wheels turning in her head as she tries to make up an excuse for why she shouldn't stay. I roll my eyes and busy myself with the pretzels, munching on them slowly so as not to make too much noise. Gabe continues to look at Jordan, smiling hopefully. He's giving her all of his attention, and it's the cutest thing ever. His head is slightly cocked, bent at an angle so he can maintain eye contact.

Jordan notices too and clears her throat again, lifting her gaze from the floor. "Yeah, I guess I can hang out down here. It is my party after all." She shrugs and laughs nervously. I squeeze her shoulder.

"Let's get this party started!" She grabs a solo cup from the table and raises it in a toast to nothing.

I pat her on the back and shake my head. "You can't pull that off." She nods and lowers the cup. "All good, though! Let's get something to fill that cup."

Gabe, Jordan, and I walk over to the kitchen, Gabe nodding to people as we pass. I watch as he fully engages in every short greeting. His eyes crinkle as his smile nearly pushes them closed. His grin is so wide that just about every tooth in his mouth is showing, every perfectly white, straight tooth. His hair flops on his forehead with every nod. I can't stop staring at him, and it's making me nervous.

 The kitchen is overflowing with people. Tim Overstript is sitting on the counter massaging Melissa Downing's shoulders. Stephanie Grantham is throwing her head back in over-dramatic laughter, clutching at Dom Jansen's arm with talon-like fingers. A bunch of kids whose names I couldn't even begin to care about are milling about having unreasonably loud conversations. I catch a glimpse of Jordan from the corner of my eye and see that she is beyond overwhelmed. I reach out to her and squeeze her hand reassuringly. She looks at me, puts her hand on my arm, and digs her nails in. Laughing, I brush her hand off.

 Gabe high fives some people and clears a spot for us at the kitchen island.

 "So, what's your poison?" He drags the various bottles of alcohol toward us - vodka, gin, rum, whiskey. I go in the fridge and grab the cranberry juice and the orange juice. Gabe points at me and nods. Heat fills my face, and I couldn't be more thankful for my dark complexion.

 Jordan taps her chin and runs her fingers up and down each bottle. "Hmm..." She looks at me, and I lift the cranberry juice bottle and motion to the vodka. "I

Sonata

guess I'll take a cranberry vodka?" Laughing, Gabe grabs a cup and unscrews the cap of the Vodka bottle.

"Are you sure about that?"

He asks, the vodka bottle poised above the cup for a generous pour. Jordan looks at me again. I nod slowly, rolling my eyes as soon as she looks away. She's always had a bad habit of relying on me in social situations. I've gotten used to it and the power dynamic it has created between us.

"Alright! Vodka Cranberry it is! How about you, my lady?"

I fan my face and giggle nervously. This whole hot-face thing is going to make the summer heat unbearable. "Yeah, I'll take the same thing. Maybe go a little easy on the vodka for Jordan's and add a splash of OJ in mine."

"I better get a tip for these custom drinks!"

He winks at me, and I almost melt. I reach past Jordan and go to push him lightly. He catches my hand and pulls me toward him. I fall into him, laughing. Jordan moves back a bit as we engage in a tickle war. I laugh despite the fact that I'm actually not ticklish. My eye catches Jordan's. She's smiling a bit but ultimately looks confused. I clear my throat and extract myself from Gabe's grasp. He's laughing and catching his breath at the same time. I straighten my shirt and grab a cup.

Three hours later and I'm on my fourth cup of cranberry vodka. Jordan, Gabe, and I have stuck together and are moving through the party as a unit. I've been downing each drink for an excuse to escape to the kitchen alone where I mix myself another drink and rest my chin in my palm to daydream about Gabe. As I stir my drink with my finger and approach Jordan and Gabe, I can't help but smile seeing them talking like old friends. Jordan is laughing at something Gabe has said and actually has her hand on his arm. If I didn't know her better, I would think she was trying to steal my man.

I stop dead in my tracks at the thought. Since when did Gabe become "my man"? Since when did I even consider having a man? My dad has always said I'm too young to date, and I never felt the need to question that or rebel against it. Dating was never on my mind, neither were boys or being conventionally pretty. None of that Cosmo magazine stuff mattered to me, but now, looking at Gabe and his deep, dark eyes, perfect teeth, and flawless olive skin, it's all I can think about. I take a huge gulp of my drink and finally join them.

"Nita! You missed the funniest thing!" Jordan grabs me with both hands, shaking me a bit. I laugh and grip my cup tighter, trying not to spill. "Sarah Dunkberth and Scott Fulsome were making out behind the door -" Jordan blushes as she recalls. "Then Dan Helms bursts in, knocking them into each other! It was hilarious! I think Scott bit Sarah's tongue!" She holds me as laughter shakes her whole body. "I wanted to help, but I couldn't stop laughing! I still can't!"

I laugh half-heartedly, a bit too distracted by these newfound feminine urges to find it funny. "What happened to them?" Looking around the room, I notice that the two are nowhere to be seen.

"Oh, they left. I don't know where they went. Probably to Sarah's house, because her mom's a nurse. She'll know what to do about her tongue!" Jordan breaks down into a fit of laughter, grabbing both Gabe and me to keep from falling. Gabe holds her up, laughing himself.

"I'm glad to see you're having fun at your own party for once!"

"Hey, I always have fun." She straightens up and pokes me in the shoulder. "This time just happens to include the actual party." Her smile softens and becomes one of utter gratitude. I squeeze her hand and nod my acceptance of the unspoken thanks.

Gabe scoots around Jordan and bumps me with his hip. "I'm surprised you're still here, Nita. What happened to your hot date?"

I grin and speak before I can think too much. "He brought me to the party." Winking, I down the rest of my drink and nod my head toward the kitchen. Gabe follows me, his hand glued to the small of my back. I giggle openly, the alcohol fully taking over.

"Another drink, my lady?" I reach my cup out toward Gabe and accept another cranberry vodka. I can't feel my face at all, but I'm having too much fun to stop drinking. Each sip is starting to taste like water and goes down just as smoothly. My insides are all warm and my sight is blurred. I can't remember ever having this much fun, but I know I probably won't remember any of it in the morning.

CHAPTER EIGHT

I wake up with the worst headache I've ever had. I groan as I sit up in a bed that's not mine. Looking around, the tension in my shoulders eases as I realize I'm in Jordan's room. Jordan is still sleeping next to me, snoring lightly. I slowly slide off the bed, trying not to disturb the mattress and wake her up. I tiptoe downstairs and grab a glass of water. The sight of the destroyed living room makes me tired and worsens my headache. Maybe if I leave before Jordan wakes up I won't have to help clean...

Before I can even finish my glass of water, Jordan is coming down the stairs. I sigh and put the glass down on the kitchen counter. I go under the sink and grab a couple of large trash bags, handing Jordan one as she approaches me. She takes it and frowns. We move through the house like cleaning zombies, groaning and shoving trash into our trash bags. When both bags are full, we plop onto the couch and lean on each other, resting our eyes.

What feels like hours go by before I open my eyes again. Jordan is laying on the armrest, still sleeping the day away. I walk to the door and give Jordan one last look before I leave. The sun is high in the sky, which means it's not too late in the day. I swing my arms as I walk home, last night's outfit still hugging my body. Yawning, I push open my front door and drag my feet up the stairs. I can hear noise in the living room, but I ignore it. I'm sure my dad didn't mind me staying over at Jordan's; he was probably glad I didn't sleep in my room with my snow globe.

The blinds in my room are open, filling the space with too much light. I squint as I close them and roll onto my bed. I dig my cell phone out of my purse and move to put it on my nightstand when I notice a text from Gabe. When did I get Gabe's number?

"Hey, Nita! Hope you didn't rage too hard after the party was over. Call me when you wake up! I have a killer hangover cure."

Sonata

I smile and tap away at the screen. "Who says I'm hungover? I happen to be an avid drinker and can really take my alcohol." Send.

I put down my phone and lay on my back, pretending to sleep. With my eyes closed, I reach over and hold my hand over my phone, waiting for it to vibrate. I'm about to fall asleep when my phone buzzes. I sit up and hold my phone inches away from my face.

"Oh, I'm sure. Can you remember anything from last night?"

I crinkle my nose and think back. Do I remember anything about last night? I remember drinking, that's for sure. We were all hanging out - Jordan, Gabe, and I. Gabe kept introducing us to a bunch of his friends, and Jordan was actually making conversation. I think I was being funny, or at least I hope I was. I remember laughing a lot and other people laughing around me. Hopefully, they weren't laughing at me. Gabe kept touching me - I remember that.

My phone buzzes again, bringing me back to the present. "You still alive over there?"

My thumbs fly across the screen. "I'm here, I'm here. As a matter of fact I don't remember much from last night. Wanna fill me in?"

Butterflies dance around in my stomach as I wait for his response. Is it presumptuous of me to assume he'd want to hang out two days in a row? I throw my phone to the corner of my bed and lay back down. I twiddle my thumbs above my stomach, the butterflies having an all-out party inside. I listen as the clock on my wall ticks the seconds away. Tick. Tick. Tick. My eye twitches slightly with every tick, each second mocking me.

After about five minutes, I head to the bathroom to take a shower and prepare for a day that may or may not be eventful. As I'm reaching for my doorknob, my phone buzzes. I turn my head but force myself to keep heading to the bathroom. I start the shower, running the hot water only, and brush my teeth as slowly and deliberately as I can muster. I let the warm water run on my face and down my body, shivering slightly with every burst of cold. I break my own record and shower in five minutes.

Leaving a trail of wet footprints, I scurry to my room without drying off. I have two texts from Gabe. I tuck the towel underneath my armpits and slide my finger across the screen.

"Sounds like a plan. I'll be at your house in 10."

"Is your dad home?"

I chew on my left thumb and tap in a response with the other. "Cool, just ring the bell. Not sure if my dad's home, I just got out of the shower." I hit send without reading it over. Is the mention of a shower too suggestive? Part of me hopes so as I slide on my cutest, matching underwear.

A minute later the doorbell rings. I wait for a few seconds and listen to see if my dad's going to get it. I don't hear anything, so I run down the stairs and throw the door open.

"I guess my dad isn't home." I attempt my most flirtatious smile but find that my lips don't move like that.

Gabe on the other hand has lips made specifically for flirtatious smiles. "How was that shower you were bragging about?"

I turn and lead him up the stairs, effectively hiding my reddening cheeks. "You know, had one shower had them all."

Gabe laughs behind me, following closely. "Not in my experience."

I continue to face forward, the subject matter of this conversation completely freaking me out. "Sounds like something worth pen paling about." I say a quick thank you to Mrs. Haim for partnering us up under my breath.

As we walk down the hall toward my bedroom, Gabe runs his hands up and down the wall. "Nita, are you taking me to your bedroom?"

Rishire Young

I walk backwards and stop at his side. "Do you want to go to my dad's room instead?"

"I have been dying to see where the great Mr. Donner rests his head." I punch him lightly on the arm and continue through my bedroom door. "So this is where the magic happens?"

I laugh. "Yeah if you count a good night's sleep as magic." It's funny how true that is.

Gabe nudges me with his shoulder. "Really depends on who that good night's sleep is with."

I let my eyes drift up from the floor and toward Gabe's face. Our eyes lock, and I'm suddenly all too aware of my hands and the fact that I have no idea what to do with them. Gabe tucks a strand of my hair behind my ear and rests his palm on my cheek. I look at his hand without moving my face, my eyes straining in their sockets. He's leaning toward me, his eyes never leaving mine. I inhale deeply, holding my breath as his lips get closer.

"Do you want to see this cool snow globe I have?!" Gabe blinks rapidly and leans away from me, surprise evident on his face.

He laughs and looks around the room. "Yeah, sure, where is it?"

I walk around him and snatch up the snow globe from my nightstand. "Here it is! My mom gave it to

Sonata

me when I was a kid. I used to have trouble sleeping. It knocks me out like that." I snap my fingers, emphasizing my point. "My dad found it a few months ago in the attic or basement or wherever with all of my mom's stuff. Did I mention she passed away last year?" I'm rambling and talking fast, the words spilling out of my mouth at a hundred miles an hour.

Gabe takes the snow globe from me, sets it back down on my nightstand, and takes my hands in his. "I am so sorry, Nita. I had no idea."

My eyes water, so I take my hands from him and wipe the tears away. I sit on my bed and wring my hands. He sits next to me and rubs my back. I look at him from the corner of my eye, inhale deeply, then lay my head on his shoulder. He scoots closer to me and hugs me to him. I breathe him in, the now familiar scent of freshly cut wood and Irish Spring body wash filling my nose and calming my nerves. I snuggle into him, and we sit there like that for a solid forty-five minutes.

After a while my neck starts to cramp, so I lean away from him, my face turned toward him. "Have you always been this nice? I feel like I would've noticed you if you had. I don't mean that as an insult." I laugh despite the tone of the situation. "I'm just finding it hard to believe that we've been neighbors this whole time, and I'm just now finding out you exist."

"Yeah, it's pretty weird." Gabe is laughing too. "Our grade is pretty big, though. To be honest, I didn't know you existed till a few months ago when all the school could talk about was your apparent disappearance. What was up with that?" His hand is still on my back, and I'm becoming more and more aware of its proximity to my butt with every passing minute.

"It was nothing. I was just in the hospital for a couple of weeks. No big deal, just some unexplainable unconsciousness or whatever." I wave my hand in the air, dismissing what could sound like a serious medical incident. I didn't mean for this whole thing to get so heavy so quickly, and all I want is to get back to flirting. "So, is that when you started stalking me and found out we're neighbors?"

Gabe nods, a smile playing at his lips. "You got me. I stalked you. I waited outside your front door for days. I had to hide in the bushes every time your dad came home. It was quite a rush."

I push him playfully. "Oh stop it! You're ridiculous."

"I feel ridiculous for not having known you longer. We've got to make up for that lost time."

I take the initiative and lean toward him. "What did you have in mind?"

Sonata

He mirrors my movement and the gap between us almost closes. "Well I could tell you, but I'd rather just show you."

Before our lips can meet in what would have been my first kiss, the front door slams shut.

"Nita! Are you home?" I jump up and just about fly to the door. I look back at Gabe and motion for him to creep behind me to the stairs. When we get to the banister, my dad is already coming up.

"Oh, I didn't know you had a guest."

I smile and put a friendly hand on Gabe's arm. "Yeah, Dad, you remember Gabe, right?" He nods, his lips in a tight smile. "I was just showing him around the house. We had just finished touring the downstairs and gotten to the upstairs bathroom when you came in." My smile is wavering, and I swallow to keep my dad from noticing.

My dad looks from me to Gabe then back to me. He smiles and joins us on the landing. "What a wonderful idea, Nita! I'll join you guys!" He claps Gabe on the back and turns us toward his bedroom. "Gabe, my man, have you seen my room yet?"

Gabe smiles and shakes his head. "No, sir. Nita figured we shouldn't go in there without you. You arrived just in time."

Rishire Young

My dad throws his head back in a boom of laughter and walks ahead of me with Gabe toward his bedroom, clearly charmed. I follow them, shaking my head at the ridiculousness of the situation.

Gabe and my dad are in front of his bed, chatting about something or other - guy stuff. I roll my eyes as I run my hand along my dad's bedspread. I walk over to his nightstand and pick up a picture of the three of us - my mom, dad, and me. My mom and dad are standing on either side of me and smiling at each other over my head. I am looking at the camera, giving my best and toothiest grin. I trace my mom's face with my index finger.

"That's a really nice picture," Gabe says from behind me. I smile without turning around. "Weren't you a cutie?"

I lean my head toward him and smile. "Are you saying I'm not cute now?"

Gabe looks over his shoulder at my dad. "Ooh, not in front of your dad." He pinches my side and joins my dad at the foot of the bed.

Sighing, I turn around and walk to the door. "Well, it doesn't seem like you guys need me here. I'll leave you two to your bonding and will be in my room if you need me."

Sonata

My dad grabs my shoulder before I can leave. "No, Sweetie, you guys hang out, I'm going to do some work in my office for a bit. It was so good seeing you again, Gabe! Come back any time!" He shakes Gabe's hand and walks past me out the door.

Gabe sidles up to me and bumps my shoulder with his. "Well that takes care of that. How about we continue where we left off in your room."

I laugh and push him away. "Come on, my dad is still too close."

Just the thought of him is too close for whatever Gabe wants to do. What does he want to do? As I walk him downstairs my mind spins with the possibilities of what he meant. My lips tingle with the idea of my first kiss. I rub my arms and swallow five, ten, a hundred times, the lump in my throat holding on to the walls of my esophagus like its nonexistent life depends on it. My eyes dart back and forth, unable to stay focused on one thing for long.

"So what do you want to do now? We can watch TV in the living room. I have the butteriest popcorn; it could clog your throat with butter."

"That sounds great and all, but I think I'm going to go home. I have a letter to write to some girl." He winks at me and turns toward the door.

Rishire Young

I follow him and hold the door open. "Well, give her my regards."

Gabe stops in the doorway and turns to me. He smiles a smile that breaks his face in half and starts to lean in. I hold my breath and wait for him to come within sniffing distance. I swallow the collection of saliva that had been gathering in my mouth and close the gap between us the way I saw in the movie Hitch, too curious to care that my dad is in the other room. My heart stops when our lips touch. His lips feel incredibly soft and full, like pillows that are attached to his face. He steps toward me and puts his hand on the back of my head, deepening the kiss.

I can feel his fingers getting tangled in my hair as his lips part mine. Our tongues meet, and it's literally the grossest and most amazing sensation I've ever experienced. A small moan-like sound escapes from my throat, and I'm afraid he's going to pull back, but he doesn't. He smiles against my lips and keeps exploring my mouth with the tip of his tongue.

He tastes like toothpaste and chocolate chip cookies, a combination that in any other circumstance would be disgusting. I think back to the wad of saliva I swallowed before the kiss and thank God I had just brushed my teeth before he came over. The minty freshness mingles in our mouths, his Colgate mixing

Sonata

with my AquaFresh. My heart hasn't started beating yet, and I feel like I could die at any moment, a happy death that I would welcome, for my lips have been kissed.

My mind is both completely blank and full to bursting. I can't feel my body; all I can feel is Gabe's tongue in my mouth. Just as I decide to hug him and make the kiss even deeper, he pulls away, smiling. I smile back, glad to see my novice kissing skills were somewhat up to par. He cocks his head to the side and sighs.

"Well, Nita Beth Donner, I guess I'll see you around."

I blink, and he's gone, the ghost of the kiss still playing on my lips. I touch them and close the door. Sliding down to the floor, I can't stop myself from feeling schoolgirl giddy. I close my eyes and smile, imagining that Gabe is still with me just waiting for another kiss. The thought of being able to kiss him again and again makes me both nervous and excited. I have to prepare; I have to always be kissing-ready; I have to get breath mints, lots and lots of breath mints.

"Dad, I'll be right back! I'm going to the store!"

CHAPTER NINE

My hands are shaking as I open my bedroom door. I drop the bag of breath mints on the floor and flop onto my bed. My eyes are stinging with fatigue, and I feel heavy all over. This day has been so long, but all I can remember is the kiss. I run my fingers along my bottom lip and smile. My lips stretch over my teeth, and I'm pretty sure I look like a deranged circus clown. I flip over to my stomach and reach for my phone. I scroll through and find what I'm looking for. I press the phone to my ear and listen to it ring.

"Hello?"

"Jordan, guess what."

"What?" She sounds exhausted.

"Are you still sleeping?" I can hear her exhaling into the mouthpiece.

"Don't judge me."

Sonata

I laugh. "I'm not judging! I wish I had slept all day, but at the same time what I did instead was pretty amazing...So, guess what."

"Am I still supposed to guess? I thought we were past that."

"Ok, party pooper, I'll just tell you. I kissed Gabe. He kissed me. Gabe and I kissed!" I hold my breath, waiting for her response.

"What?" I can practically hear her rubbing her eyes.

"Can't you hear me?!" How can she not be paying attention? This is kind of a big deal! I'm about to hang up when she starts gasping.

"Oh. My. Gosh. What?! What?!?! You guys did what?! Nita, oh my gosh, your first kiss! Oh my gosh! Can I come over?!"

I sit up and bounce on my bed happy that she's just as excited as I am. "Yes, please! Come right now!"

She squeals, almost bursting my eardrums, and hangs up the phone without another word. I hold the phone to my chest and kick my legs. My phone buzzes against my sternum. I hold it up to my face and smile even wider. Gabe.

"Hey there." I love how he punctuates his texts. He totally doesn't have to! It's like he's writing me a very short letter. Speaking of letters...

"How's that letter coming along? I hope you're waxing poetic. You know how much girls love waxing." I can't help but laugh at my cleverness.

"Good one. My letter is coming along great; thanks for asking. I think she's gonna like it."

"Are you going to tell me who this mystery girl is?" The thing I love about texting is being able to think my responses through. I don't feel this confident in person, and my movie quoting is off the charts in the messenger app.

"Oh, I don't think you know her. She's beautiful, funny, head in the clouds, basically always asleep on her feet."

I giggle to myself, thankful for the walls and lawn that separate us.

"She sounds like a real winner. Tell me, what are your intentions for this young lady?" I bite my lip, hoping not to come off like a desperate schoolgirl with a moon-sized crush. Another good thing about texting - ambiguous tones. I could always argue a different meaning if I have to save my skin. If I could give the person who invented texting a hug, I would give him a kiss, you know, now that I know how to do that.

The doorbell rings, and I jump to my feet to get it. Running down the stairs, I practically fly to the door.

Sonata

Jordan lunges at me as soon as I get the door open, and we fall backwards a bit in a clumsy embrace.

"Nita, I'm so excited for you! You have a boy--" I shove my fingers onto her lips, shushing her. I grab her arm and half drag her up the stairs to my room.

"I don't want my dad to know! He's pretty comfortable with having Gabe over when he's not home, and I want it to stay that way. Plus, I don't want to jinx anything. It's not like anything's official yet. We just kissed..." Jordan puts her hands on her hips, a smirk on her face.

"You're telling me a boy and a girl would kiss and not be boyfriend and girlfriend? Puh-lease, Nita! That's not how that thing works. He obviously likes you, and you obviously like him. You guys are dating! Deal with it."

"Jordan." I put my hand on her shoulder in an overly condescending way. "Gabe and I haven't even been on a date. How can you say we're dating?"

She shakes me off and sits on the edge of my bed. "Wouldn't you guys coming to my party together count as a date?"

I scratch my head and squint off to the side. "Maybe...I don't know! It's not like he specifically said *'Hey, Nita, want to go to Jordan's party as my date?'*. Plus, we're neighbors, so it only made sense that we walked over together." Despite my arguments, part of me thinks Jordan might be right. What if last night was a date? What if Gabe thinks we're boyfriend and girlfriend, and I'm over here not acting like a girlfriend?!

At the same time, what if we're wrong, and I mess everything up by being weird and girlfriend-y? It's not like Gabe and I have had any kind of conversation about this. I don't even know how one of those would go. My head is spinning in confusion, and I'm dreading seeing Gabe again for fear of doing something stupid. I plop down next to Jordan and sigh loudly, my whole body shaking with the exhalation.

"What am I going to do?!" Jordan opens her mouth to speak, and I hold up my finger, shushing her again. "Forget I asked - you giving me advice is like the blind leading the blind." Jordan frowns slightly. I put my hand on hers. "No offense."

She shrugs. "None taken. You're totally right. Neither of us have any experience with this stuff, but you know who does?"

I nod excitedly. "When's she coming back?"

Jordan squeals. "Not till the end of summer! She went backpacking in the Appalachian mountains with her roommates as soon as school ended."

I lay back on the bed, my hands landing beside me in a thud. "She's so freaking cool. You're so lucky you have an older sister. I would give anything to have a sibling."

Jordan snuggles up to me and kisses my shoulder. "Nita, you know I'm basically your sister. And I'm two months older than you, so it's like I'm your older sister."

"Keep telling yourself that," I say laughing. "Hey, is Jackie going to be throwing a coming home/end of the summer party when she gets back?"

"That's a great question. I bet she is just so she can tell all her friends how her freshman year was. You know how she likes to brag."

My eyebrows furrow, wrinkling my forehead. "What does she have to brag about? I'm pretty sure all of her friends had freshman years."

Jordan laughs shortly. "Yeah, but she's the only one who got out of this town. She's going to want to talk about big city living, although she only went to Boston, not New York City or Chicago."

"I love Jackie! She's ridiculous!" I laugh.

Jordan struggles to push me in her lying down position. "You better not love her more than you love me!"

I laugh again and give her a side hug that's more me hugging the bed. With my head on her shoulder, I can't stop smiling and feeling like my old self again. I haven't thought about using the snowglobe since school ended, and that both scares and excites me. Of course I still miss my mom, but I feel like things are finally starting to pick up, and get back to normal.

My phone vibrates beside me. I had almost forgotten that I texted Gabe about his intentions. I'm nervous to read his response, the look on my face making it glaringly obvious to Jordan who puts a hand on my shoulder and cocks her head to the side questioningly. I ignore her and swipe through to my messages. A smile slowly creeps across my face and a monosyllabic giggle escapes my lips.

"Well I could tell you, but I'd rather just show you..." A kissy face emoji caps off the text that stops my heart.

The next day starts just the way I like my days to start - with the smell of bacon and eggs. I go downstairs still in my pajamas, my teeth unbrushed, and slide into a seat at the dining table. Right on cue, my dad puts a plate of scrambled eggs and bacon in front of me. I grab a bowl of fruit - orange and apple slices, strawberries, and blueberries - and go to town on this borderline gourmet breakfast.

Sonata

"Dad, this is delicious! What's the occasion?" The words come out through a wall of partially chewed food, a few drops of spit flying out of my mouth and onto my plate.

"Does there have to be a special occasion for me to make breakfast for my amazing daughter?"

I stop, the fork hovering in front of my mouth. I look at him through narrowed eyes and lower the fork to my plate. I cross my arms over my chest and push back from the table, still staring at my dad. He's avoiding my gaze, shoveling forkfuls of eggs into his mouth. I clear my throat and cross my legs underneath the table, jostling it a bit. He finally looks up at me and smiles. I raise my eyebrows, the silence surrounding us.

"So how was your day yesterday? I saw that Jordan came over, and that Gabe guy was here. Looks like it's shaping up to be quite a fun summer."

I know what this is about. He's glad I'm still here, that I'm still awake. He sees my friends coming over as a sign that I'm going to stay. Now he doesn't have to go back on his promise, but he also doesn't have to fulfill it. I cross my arms even tighter, anger rising in my chest.

After about a minute, I stand and take the plate to the living room where I continue to eat, watching an episode of New Girl. I can hear my dad eating in the dining room, his fork clinking against his plate every time he scoops up some eggs. The bacon crunches in my mouth, the perfect amount of crispiness. I keep the volume low on the TV, the episode not interesting enough to pay attention to. My mind is going a thousand miles a minute, bouncing from one feeling to the next - anger at my dad and his lack of commitment to his promise, confusion at my anger considering how happy I am to be awake, sadness that I haven't thought about using the snow globe or even much about my mom in any conscious way.

As soon as I empty my plate I shut off the TV and walk to the kitchen, passing the now empty dining room. I wash the dishes, the scalding hot water burning my hands through the gloves. My eyes ache with fatigue, and I'm wondering if I should go back to sleep. I am still in my pajamas after all. I slink up the stairs practically on my hands and knees and roll back into bed. As soon as I close my eyes, my phone rings.

Without opening my eyes, I answer the phone. "Hello?"

"Well hello there, Sleeping Beauty. I'm assuming you're still in bed."

Sonata

My eyes fly open, and I sit up, my back as straight as a rod. "Gabe! Hi! I'm not still in bed!" I stand to make it true. "What's up?"

Gabe laughs on the other end. "I was thinking we could hang out. I know we've seen each other every day since classes ended, but I figured since we're neighbors, hanging out is just a walk across the driveway."

I rifle through my dresser for a tank top, holding my phone between my ear and my shoulder. I shimmy out of my pajama pants and pull on a pair of cuffed jean shorts. "What did you have in mind?" I put the call on speaker and clasp on my bra underneath my pajama shirt. Pulling the shirt over my head, I grab a jewel-toned green top and lay it on my bed, running my hand along it to smooth out the wrinkles.

"I noticed you have quite the swing set in your backyard. I'm thinking, a little jump competition." I pull the shirt over my head and snatch up the phone, turning off speaker mode. "Sounds like a plan, but I've got to warn you, I've got some pretty good swing skills."

Gabe's laugh is like music to my ears. "Challenge accepted! I'll meet you by the back fence in twenty minutes - give you a chance to get out of bed."

Rishire Young

"Shut up!" I hang up without waiting for a response, hoping it comes off flirtatious and not rude.

I'm thankful for the time, though. I rush to the bathroom and splash some water on my face in an attempt to wake myself up. I brush my teeth longer than necessary and even floss, something I only do right before a dental appointment. Back in my room, I slip on a pair of tan Havaianas and stride out the back door as coolly as I can so as not to seem too eager in case he can see me from his house.

The sun is casting an almost heavenly glow on the swing set as I approach. The whole thing creaks when I sit down, giving me a real confidence boost. I kick my legs back and forth, rising higher and higher. With my head thrown back, I start to get really dizzy and almost fall out of the swing. A knock on the gate forces me upright. I walk over to the gate and let him in.

"Ready to lose?" Gabe says with a smirk.

He squeezes my shoulder and walks past me to the swing. I follow behind him, close but not too close. He sits on the swing and starts kicking his feet, rising higher and higher in the air. I join him on the other seat and push off with all of my might. We laugh as we swing our legs harder and harder.

Sonata

He reaches his hand out and grabs a hold of my swing, slowing me down a bit. "Hey, no cheating!" I reach for his swing and catch a handful of air. He laughs as he continues to hold onto my swing. "Hey!"

I'm leaning toward his swing, reaching my arms out as far as I can, but I can't get a hold of the chain links. I wiggle in the seat and start to swing side-to-side instead of back-and-forth. My momentum shifts, and I start bumping into him, forcing him to swing side-to-side.

"Whoa!"

He lets go of my swing and holds onto his own. I laugh as I continue to bump into him. He starts bumping into me, and before I know it, we're bumping into each other simultaneously, throwing us to extreme ends of the swing set. In the blink of an eye we're on the floor, rolling toward each other and laughing.

"You're crazy, you know that?" Gabe squeezes my forearm, his laughter filling my ears.

"Hey, I wasn't the one who started it! You were grabbing my swing first!"

I sit and wheeze a bit as I laugh. The air is fighting to get out of my lungs, and I feel like I'm blowing out of a thin straw. Breathing turns into coughing, and tears are streaming down my face as I struggle to exhale.

Gabe pats me on the back, concern stretching across his face. "Are you ok?"

I continue to cough, the pressure in my chest lessening. I inhale deeply and swallow the pool of saliva that had been collecting in my mouth. "Yeah, I'm alright. The fall just knocked the wind out of me."

He continues to pat my back, the patting turning into a sort of massage. "Well, take it easy. How about we go inside, get you a glass of water?"

I grab his hand to stand and nod as we walk through my backdoor. Sitting on the couch, I turn on the TV while I wait for Gabe to return with a glass of water. I switch from Animal Planet to a Law & Order: SVU marathon on USA Network. I slide down on the couch and bring my knees to my chest, wrapping my arms around my legs.

Gabe bounds in with two glasses of water, the water almost spilling as he sets the cups on the table. He puts his arm around me and hands me a glass. I take a long sip and put the glass down immediately, wanting my hands free to grab his neck and pull him closer to me as we kiss.

Just as I'm thinking of kissing him, he leans in, his eyes already partially closed. I smile and lean in too, meeting him halfway. His lips are as soft as I remember. My mind goes blank as his tongue enters my

Sonata

mouth. He wraps his arms around me and pulls me into him. I fall into his chest, our mouths still connected like suction cups. I run my fingers through his hair and hold his face in my hands, his cheeks warm against my palms.

We stay this way for at least ten minutes. When we finally come up for air, my lips are numb and my tongue is dry from giving him all of my saliva. I laugh as I lift the cup of water to my mouth and take a nice, long sip. He puts his hand on my thigh as he reaches for his cup. I put my hand on his and intertwine our fingers.

A new episode of SVU comes on, and we snuggle against each other, his back on the armrest, mine on his chest. The episode unfolds in front of us, neither of us paying much attention to the case. My mind is wandering, thinking about the kiss we just shared and our first kiss and the kisses we'll share in the future. He sighs behind me, the sound rumbling in his chest and making me vibrate. When a commercial break comes on, I turn in my seat and look at him. He smiles at me, his eyes questioning my sudden movement.

"So, I've been thinking."

"Mmhmm." His eyes never leave mine.

"I really like kissing you." I'm blushing like crazy, my face so hot I'm afraid it's going to melt off. "I have

to admit I'm a bit new to this whole thing. Are we...."
Before I can get the words out, the front door swings open.

Gabe and I jump apart and land on opposite sides of the couch. My dad comes in and stops at the entrance to the living room. "Hey, Dad." I nod at him nonchalantly, my head resting on my hand.

"Hey, Mr. Donner. How's it going?" My dad approaches Gabe, and they clap hands like college bros.

"What's up, Gabe, my man?! How's it hanging?"

I laugh, almost spitting all over the couch. "*How's it hanging? Who are you?*"

My dad rolls his eyes and starts walking backwards. "Whatever. I'll see you cool kids later. I'll be in my office doing some work. Holler at me if you need anything!"

I practically choke, I'm laughing so much. "Ok, Dad! We'll holler!" He leaves, and I look at Gabe, rolling my eyes.

"You're dad is such a nut!"

"You're telling me." I lean on him as we laugh.

"What were you going to say?"

I bite my lip and hold my knees to my chest. I look at him from the corner of my eye. Should I really ask him if we're going out? Is that something people do? Will he think I'm a total weirdo noob? What if he's

Sonata

about to ask me to be his girlfriend, and I'm stepping on his toes? Guys don't like that, right? It's, like, emasculating, isn't it? Ugh, I can't do this! My dad totally messed up the moment!

"It was nothing. I totally forgot!" I bop myself on the head and laugh.

He reaches over and shakes my arm. "You're a nut, too, ya know."

I punch him lightly on the arm and give him a quick kiss on the lips. We settle into each other and turn our attention back to the TV just in time to see a woman bleeding out in an alley.

CHAPTER TEN

Although it feels like Gabe is occupying all of the space in my brain even after such a short time, I'm finding myself back in a place where I'm actually free to be happy, which leads me to Jordan's front porch. As I wait for her to let me in, I take in my surroundings. It feels like forever since things looked this bright. It's like I've been looking down ever since my mom died, and now that I'm looking up, I like what I see. I like how the world looks with what can only be called the rose colored glasses of a teenage crush.

Jordan swings the front door open with aplomb. Her arms sweep toward the foyer, inviting me to enter. I laugh as I walk past her. As soon as she closes the door, she throws her arm over my shoulder and practically drags me up the stairs to her room. Once inside, she shuts the door then turns to face me dramatically. I back into her bed and sit down with a bounce, a small smile playing on my lips.

Sonata

"Don't just sit there! Spill! What's it like dating the literal boy next door?"

I lean back on my hands and shrug casually. Despite my desire to play it cool, a squeal escapes my lips, which launches Jordan onto the bed.

"I don't want to talk about it!" I'm holding her back as she tries to shake it out of me. "Stop it, Jordan, you're going to jinx it!"

I can't help but smile, though, because as much as I don't want to admit it, I'm beyond excited to be dating the boy next door, even if we're not really, technically dating. Whatever it is that we're doing, I like it alot and want to talk about it alot, but I really don't want to jinx it, because, like I said, I like it, alot.

Jordan rolls her eyes and lays back on the bed. I join her, and we turn our heads to look at each other. It reminds me of when we were kids and would have a sleepover every weekend. We would build a fort out of her sheets and lay on pillows, telling silly stories and giggling. Our moms would be sitting right outside of our fort, drinking wine and talking in hushed tones. We didn't pay them any mind - we were always so lost in our own worlds.

Together, our imaginations constantly transported us to places that I had forgotten about till now. We used to slay dragons and be heroes just like every other kid, but somehow it felt different, more real. It was like our brains were operating on another level that let us see what we believed. Thinking about it now, it actually reminds me a bit of my dream-comas.

It's not like we were asleep when we played like this nor did we ever walk through the back of an enchanted closet, but the imaginary lives that we created for ourselves were so intricate and detailed that they seemed almost tangible - not nearly as tangible as the dream-comas are, but close enough that I feel like Jordan might be the only person who would really understand what's happening.

"Jordan, do you remember when we were kids, and we would have the wildest adventures? I remember this one time, we transformed the woods by the park into an amusement park and rode rides all afternoon. I don't know about you, but I could legit feel the wind in my hair as if I were on an actual rollercoaster. Do you remember that?" My gaze is hopeful as I wait for her response. It's been a while since Jordan and I have really talked, but something about this afternoon and the way it feels just like old times makes me think that I can tell her anything and not get hurt.

I can see the wheels turning in Jordan's head as she tries to remember. A huge smile breaks out across her face when the memory lands. "Those were the best

Sonata

times! I remember everything feeling so real. I would tell Jackie about it, and she always called me crazy!" She laughs, rolling her eyes. "It felt like a secret that only you and I shared, ya know. No one else understood, but we had each other, so it didn't matter." Sadness casts a shadow over her face, which clenches my heart.

Wiggling closer to her in our laying down positions, I grab her hand and squeeze gently. "I have another secret for you." Jordan squeezes my hand back, biting her lip to keep from interrupting. "So, you know how I was missing weeks of school a few months ago?" She nods, her eyes slowly widening. "Well, I was in a coma..." A gasp tumbles out of her mouth. She claps her hands over it and nods for me to continue.

"That day we skipped maybe five seconds of school, the day of the six month anniversary of the accident, my dad found my snowglobe - you know that one of Rockefeller Center." She nods again, her hands still over her mouth. "When I got home after school, he gave it to me, and of course I turned it on. Like usual, it knocked me right out, but when I woke up, I was in another universe I think." She furrows her eyebrows, confusion evident on the parts of her face that I can see beyond her hand. "In this other world or universe or whatever, my mom is alive…"

"What?!" The word explodes from her mouth, her hands flying out toward me. "How is that possible?! What do you mean she's alive? Is this some sort of physics kind of thing where we have multiple universes or were you maybe hallucinating?"

I shake my head and shrug. "You see, I don't know! I don't know anything! All I do know is that whenever I use the snowglobe in this world, I wake up in that world, and one day in that world is a whole week in this world. Maybe I'm having the most lucid dream ever, because I get to do stuff in that world. I get to talk to my mom, touch her, hang out with her. It feels as real as you and me talking right now. I don't know how to describe it…"

"Nita, that's…" My heart does butterfly kicks in my chest as I wait for her to continue. "Amazing."

I let go of the breath that I didn't realize I had been holding. Her eyes are shining with barely restrained tears that cause my eyes to well up in response. She strokes my arm and smiles serenely, like I just told her the secret to happiness, and she's absorbing it. A tear escapes my eyes, and I laugh as I wipe it away.

"This is honestly the coolest thing I've ever heard. It's almost like you willed your mom back to life." It

Sonata

feels amazing getting this off my chest and not being treated like I'm crazy. Jordan's reaction is beyond my wildest dreams, and I couldn't be more grateful to have her in my life right now.

"It would be a lot better if I didn't have to be in a coma." I can't help but laugh at the absurdity of this whole thing. Jordan laughs too, although there's an apprehension in her eyes that makes me want to take it all back. "Just so we're clear, the doctor said that the comas are harmless." She nods but doesn't look any more reassured.

I shrug it off, wanting to get back to her being amazed and not worried. "Anyway, that world is just like this world, but I've only really interacted with my mom in it. We see kids and parents at the park, but I haven't seen my dad or you yet. I've only gone there a couple of times, though, so who knows who I will meet!"

Jordan's genuine smile returns as she rests her head in the palm of her hand. "So, when are you going back?"

I shift in the bed so that I'm laying on my stomach and look out the window. This whole conversation made me forget about Gabe, if only for a few moments. Now, thinking about taking a week long nap, he's back to being front and center of my mind. A silly smile creeps across my face as I think about kissing him.

"What's got you smiling like that?" Jordan is smirking at me, her eyebrows raised conspiratorially.

I duck my head down to hide my grin then roll over onto my back to stare at the ceiling. "To tell you the truth, Jordan, my dad gave me permission to spend the whole summer in this other world." Her eyes widen in shock. I nod, pursing my lips. "But ever since I started hanging out with Gabe..."

"Don't you mean dating Gabe?" She wiggles her eyebrows, making me laugh.

"Whatever it is that we're doing, I'm having so much fun doing it that I haven't even thought much about using the snowglobe and spending time in the other world." Jordan's mouth falls open in surprise. "Don't get me wrong, I still miss my mom like crazy, but it's not the only thing that I think about...Is that bad?"

Jordan sits up and scoots closer to me. I sit up too, facing her. She reaches out and takes my hand, rubbing it between hers. "Nita, there's nothing wrong with moving on. You're allowed to think about more than one thing, even if that one thing is as huge as missing your mom." A tear slides down my cheek. Jor-

Sonata

dan wipes it away with her thumb then rests her hand on my cheek. "You deserve happiness, Nita."

I nod against her hand. "It's just weird, because the way I miss my mom right now is how I would miss her if she were just on a trip, you know. Having this power to see her and speak to her makes it feel like she never died..."

Jordan nods, her hand still on my cheek. "But she did, Nita...." My eyes lock on hers as they fill with tears. With her hand on my cheek, she catches them as they fall.

When I get home, I'm emotionally exhausted. Falling back into old patterns with Jordan, we talked about any and everything. It felt so good to confide in her and to have my friend back in a real way. Being with Gabe has made me feel like my old self again, and I couldn't be happier.

Walking into the living room, I find my dad lounging on the couch, the TV playing a true crime documentary on mute. I plop down next to him, snuggling his arm. He puts it around me and squeezes. I shift on the couch, turning to face him. He does the same, his head falling to one side in curiosity.

"Why are you sitting on the couch letting the TV watch you?"

A small smile brightens his face as he shakes his head. "I was watching TV then started thinking about stuff. The TV got distracting, so I muted it."

I take his large hand in my small ones and hold it in my lap. "What are you thinking about, Dad?"

He shrugs and looks up, searching for his thoughts. "I wish I could read your mind," he says, returning his gaze to my eyes.

Laughing, I raise my eyebrows. "So you were thinking about having superpowers?"

He laughs too, the sound somehow hollow. "No, silly girl. I just wish I knew what you were thinking. I wish I knew how your mind worked, especially with these comas..."

I sink into the couch, unsure as to how to respond. Truthfully, I don't know how my mind works while I'm in the comas either. I don't know what to tell my dad that will make him feel better. All I know is that these comas make me feel better. Can't that be enough?

"I really don't know what to tell you, Dad. I'm sorry..." The look of dejection on his face squeezes my heart. After such a cathartic day with Jordan, I don't have the mental or emotional bandwidth to tend to my dad's feelings. As bad as it sounds, I can't hold

Sonata

both of our emotions. He's going to have to hold his own.

I stand and head toward the stairs. "Nita, wait!" I keep going, on a mission to hold on to what was once a good day. "I didn't mean to upset you! It's just that I wake up every day, wondering if this will be the day you decide to use the snowglobe. I don't know what you're thinking, and I want so desperately to understand..."

I stop at the top of the stairs and look down at him in the foyer. I can see it in his eyes that he wants more - more of me, more of an explanation, more than I can give right now.

"Dad, it's fine. I'm beat. I'll see you in the morning." I turn on my heels and make it into my bedroom before he has the time to respond. I flop onto my bed and whip out my phone, dialing without much thought. After a couple of rings, Gabe answers, his voice the very thing I need to hear right now.

"Hey." I can hear him smiling. "I've been thinking about you."

I sit up and lean on my headboard, twirling a piece of hair around my finger. "Oh, yeah? What were you thinking?"

He laughs, the sound so intoxicating that I feel dizzy. "Just that I missed you today. What'd you do?"

Rishire Young

"Missed you." I walk over to my window and look out toward Gabe's house. The lights in his bedroom are on, but the blinds are down, so I can't see inside. I rest my hand on the cool glass, wondering if he's sitting on the bed right now or maybe sitting at his desk, doodling our initials.

"I guess we did the same thing today, then. Wish we had done it together."

I absentmindedly draw hearts in the condescension in the window. "Me too, but I had to spend time with Jordan. She's my best friend."

"I get it! We don't have to be joined at the hip, but just know that when we're apart, I'm always thinking about you."

I bite my lip to keep from squealing. My heart is doing flips in my chest, and a whole butterfly garden has sprouted in my stomach. "That's really sweet, Gabe. I'm always thinking about you, too."

Leaning on the wall, I turn my head so that I can still see Gabe's house. A shadow moves across his window, and the light goes out in his bedroom. I hear him sigh on the other end. "You sound tired. You should get some sleep." I don't want this conversation to end, but I want to be considerate.

He laughs again, tickling my eardrums. "You can tell over the phone, huh?"

Sonata

I laugh, too. "Just goes to show that I know you pretty well, Gabe Hilstone."

"Well, then, goodnight, Nita Beth Donner. See you tomorrow?"

I nod although he can't see me. I imagine him watching me through his blinds like I'm watching his dark room. I imagine him fantasizing about when we'll see each other again, touch each other again, kiss each other again, just like I am. Looking back at my bed, I imagine him sleeping next to me, our bodies intertwined as we dream side by side.

"It's a date." This summer is shaping up to be a good one.

CHAPTER ELEVEN

Just as I thought, this has been one of the best summers that I can remember. I've spent just about every day with Gabe - hanging out at my place, chilling at his, and going to parties I would never have been invited to if I hadn't been hanging out with Gabe. I drag Jordan along with us to the parties, so I'm getting the best of both worlds.

Despite the crazy amount of time we've been spending together, Gabe hasn't brought up what I almost brought up that time on the couch. I still don't know if we're officially dating. Is he seeing other people? Should I be seeing other people? How would I even go about seeing other people?! I barely have time to see my bed!

Speaking of my bed, I can't believe I've gone this long without thinking about the snow globe. As each day goes by and I continue to wake up in the real world, I'm forgetting what it's like to be in that dream

Sonata

world with my mom and the recurring trip to the park. I can tell my dad is anxious but happy. He makes me breakfast every morning, and I've stopped emotionally rebelling against his indirect retraction of his promise. Everything is going great, and it's honestly scaring me a bit.

As I wait for Gabe to come over so that we can head out on a maybe-date, I sit on my bed and stare at the snow globe. I consider taking a little nap, a little week long nap, but I really don't want to miss an afternoon with Gabe, kissing on the couch and talking till my tongue falls asleep. I blink back tears as I run my fingers along the winding key.

The doorbell rings, and my heart lifts in my chest. I smile against the tears that are escaping from my eyes. Putting the snow globe back on my nightstand, I race down the stairs and throw the door open, greeting Gabe with a hug that's more like a tackle.

He laughs into my hair, his breath making my scalp tingle. We intertwine fingers as we make our way down the street toward the ice cream parlor. His hand is cool in mine, counteracting the summer heat that accompanies us. I keep my eyes trained ahead of me so as not to be caught staring although all I want to do is drink him up like an ice cold lemonade on this scorcher of a day. We stop at a corner, and he takes that moment to turn to me and gently caress my cheek, a move that I have found to be a precursor to a nice, long kiss.

I bite my lower lip and tilt my head like I've seen girls do in just about every romantic comedy. His mouth is on mine before I can think of what to do next, and I'm more than happy for the distraction. I hook my free arm on his neck, deepening the kiss. This public display of affection is so decadent that the thought of ice cream makes my stomach turn a bit.

As the minutes tick by while we're lip locked, I can't help but think that he's claiming me. Right here, in the middle of our neighborhood, potentially surrounded by people we know, he's kissing me with a reckless abandon that we had previously reserved for my bedroom. This is a lot better than a conversation about what we are, I can tell you that much.

After what feels like hours, we finally come up for air. Gabe licks his lips, probably wanting to taste me one last time. I wipe my mouth with the back of my hand, feeling a bit self conscious all of a sudden. A nervous giggle tumbles out of my mouth, and I move to continue toward the ice cream parlor. We swing our interwoven hands as we saunter down the street toward a sweet treat, the literal ice cream on top of the cake that was that kiss.

Sonata

A bell above the door rings as we enter the shop, signaling our arrival. In a corner, I see a few of Gabe's friends laughing in a booth. I've seen these guys more this summer than I have all school year. I guess you could say they're my friends, too!

They wave us over, and I'm awash in excitement. I feel like I belong, with Gabe's palm flush against mine. He releases my hand to drape his arm over my shoulder when we reach the table. He fist bumps the guys and waggles his eyebrows at the girls. I lift my hand in a little wave, hoping to come off cooler than I feel. Melanie Frell pats the seat beside her and smiles up at me.

"Sit down, babe. I'll grab us some ice cream. Mint chocolate chip, right?"

I sit next to Melanie and nod. "With a waffle cone, please!"

Gabe bows dramatically. "Anything for my lady." The group laughs, and I can feel my face heating up.

"Girl, you two are so cute!" Melanie exclaims, squeezing my hand.

"You are so lucky you bagged a guy like Gabe, Nita. He is beyond fine." Sabrina winks at me from across the table, and I feel like I'm in a scene from Mean Girls, except the girls are anything but mean.

Rishire Young

"I would say I'm the lucky one." Gabe returns in the nick of time, saving me from having to come up with a witty response.

He slides into the booth beside me and hands me an ice cream cone. I maintain eye contact as I slide my tongue around the circumference of the scoop. He reaches over and puts his finger on my chin, tilting my head up. He licks a glob of ice cream off my lips, sending shockwaves through my body.

A chorus of ooohs erupts around us. Braeden and Kyle shove at Gabe, knocking him into me. I clutch my ice cream cone tightly, nearly dropping it on my lap. The girls and I laugh as Gabe and the guys continue to rough house.

I savor my ice cream as Melanie, Sabrina, and Kitty talk over each other. I laugh at the appropriate times to show that I'm paying attention, but I'm too wrapped up in my own thoughts to really listen.

I feel like a real teenage girl for the first time in my life. I'm sitting at what could only be called the popular table despite the fact that it's in the corner of an ice cream parlor and not the middle of a cafeteria, being included in conversation and making memories. There's a hot guy sitting next to me, absent-mindedly holding my hand as he holds court with his friends.

Sonata

My hair is actually cooperating today, and I look pretty cute. I'm living the dream!

Strangely enough, it's the only dream I've been thinking about this summer. I drift off to sleep every night going over my day, which plays out like an early 2000s high school sitcom. I wake up excited to star in my own episode of 90210, minus the rich kids and obscene lack of parental guidance. My days are booked and busy with social events that leave me little time to think of much else, and I've been loving every minute of it, that is, until something reminds me of the piece of my heart that's missing.

"My mom has been on my case lately. She made me give her the password to my laptop, and she uses it to read my iMessages! Kyle and I have had to switch to using WhatsApp to communicate, but I make sure we have something innocent for her to read. She doesn't know that I know that she's basically spying on me. She's so annoying. I legit hate her." Sabrina stabs at her sundae to make her point, causing the cherry to sink to the bottom.

Melanie and Kitty nod their agreement. The three girls turn to look at me expectantly then with widened eyes, reach over to me, stroking different parts of my arm. "Nita, I'm so sorry that I said that! I don't hate my mom. I know I'm just lucky to have her. I'm so sorry to make you think about your mom."

I shrug, trying to look as nonchalant as possible. I hate the way they're looking at me right now, with all of this pity like I'm someone to be treated differently. It reminds me of sessions with Mrs. Miskole, and all of a sudden I'm no longer living any kind of dream. I shrug again, unable to come up with anything to say and afraid that if I did say something, I would start crying right then and there. I busy myself with polishing off my ice cream cone. The crunch of the last bite eases my discomfort. My feelings go down my throat along with the cone.

Melanie, Sabrina, and Kitty have already moved on, and just like that, I'm no longer the focus of their attention. I seize that moment to excuse myself to the bathroom. Once inside the single stall, I finally exhale. I never know what to do in that kind of situation when my grief is center stage. In my defense, I never thought I would be in a situation where a group of people are talking to me. Social etiquette was never my strong suit, and it got a lot weaker when I basically stopped talking after the accident.

I splash some water on my face then flush the toilet for good measure. When I walk out of the stall, I almost run into Gabe who is waiting for me.

Sonata

"Hey. Are you alright? The girls told me what they said. I'm sorry, Nita."

I shrug again, my shoulders getting more of a workout in the past ten minutes than they have my whole life. "Seriously, it's not a big deal. I get how Sabrina feels. I watch TV; I know what an annoying mother is like, at least in theory. You all don't have to treat me any differently just because I don't have one." The last sentence catches in my throat, and my eyes start to water against my will. I look up and curse my overactive tear ducts.

Gabe strokes my arms then pulls me into him. He rubs my back and places soft kisses on my neck. I lean back and smile at him, his concern melting my heart. He smiles back and caresses my cheek. Instead of our usual, passionate kiss, he simply brushes my lips with his before leading me back to the table.

"Hey, guys. Nita and I are gonna head out. We'll see you all next week at Steve's place."

I grab my purse from the chair. Melanie takes my hand before I can turn to leave. "Nita, I'm sorry if we made you feel uncomfortable. We love having you in the group! Hope we didn't mess that up with our big mouths."

I squeeze her hand and look each of them in the eye. "It's really no big deal. Today was really fun. I'll see you all next week!" She squeezes my hand back then lets go. Gabe puts his hand on the small of my back and leads me out the door. We interlock our fingers and walk to my place.

As soon as we get through my front door, I grab his hand and lead him upstairs to my bedroom. Gratitude fills me as I recall his look of concern when I came out of the bathroom. I just know he feels the same way about me that I feel about him. He snakes his arms around my waist and pushes me against the door as soon as I close it. Laughing, I rest my head on the door and watch as Gabe leans toward me, his lips poised for kissing. I wrap my arms around his neck and lose myself in what I'm sure is the best kiss anyone's ever had.

"You're an amazing kisser." Gabe says, tucking a strand of hair behind my ear.

I blush and bite my lip. This month has been crazy, and I feel like a completely different person. Spending all this time with Gabe has really leveled up my kissing game, and although we haven't specified what we are, I've been going around thinking that I'm his girlfriend. Girlfriend feels so good to say and makes my whole body tingle. I wonder if he feels the same way about being my boyfriend.

Sonata

I run my hand up and down his arm, grab his index finger, and walk him to my bed. We sit down, facing each other, staring into each other's eyes, and completely absorbing each other. I want to capture everything about Gabe - his gorgeous full lips, his deep, dark eyes, his flawless olive skin.

As my eyes feast on his features, I can't help but think that I'm falling in love with this boy. I know we haven't been seeing each other for that long. I'm not even sure that what we've been doing can be considered "seeing each other" since he hasn't said anything about us being official. Why does he get to make that decision? Oh, right, because I'm too chicken to ask. That's the way it works, though, right? The guy defines the relationship, and I just take what I can get when I can get it?

I prided myself on not being like other girls - all dreamy about boys and obsessive - but with Gabe, I just can't help it! He's so cute and nice and funny, and I really love kissing him! That means I love him, right? Whatever it means, I can't say anything to anyone, at least not until he says something first.

We've been staring at each other in silence for the longest time, and I have no idea what to say. The creepiest smile is forming on my face, and I've basically forgotten how to interact with another human being. How long has it been since one of us said something? Should I be the first one to speak? What is there to talk about?

"So, do you want to hang out tonight? My dad is working late in the city, so we'll have the whole house to ourselves." I smile as seductively as I can.

"Oh, I would, but I have to stay home and do some summer reading. My mom has been on my case about it, since I've been spending so much time with you."

My eyes widen to the size of saucers. "No! Your mom hates me?! I should talk to her! Maybe we can do our summer reading together, then she can see that I really care about school!"

Gabe laughs, which is weird, since this is a really serious situation. I can't have the love of my life's mom hate me! That would ruin our relationship!

"Calm down, Nita! She doesn't hate you; she just wants me to stay in tonight. We can hang out tomorrow night. It's no big deal."

I nod even though I think it's a huge deal.

"That's cool. Tomorrow then. Hey, I could stand to stay in and do some summer reading too." In fact, I can surprise him, and we can do the summer reading together. And by "summer reading" I mean making out. Maybe some summer reading too; I actually haven't cracked open a book this whole summer.

Sonata

He stands up, and I follow him to the front door. Leaning on the door, he moves toward me and gives me the sweetest, smallest kiss on the lips. My eyes flutter open as he strides down the driveway. He doesn't even turn around to make eye contact one last time. Part of me finds that to be kind of rude, but the other part thinks it's kind of mysterious and sexy.

It's not until after seven that I decide to go over to Gabe's house. I walk across our adjoining lawn, holding The Sound and The Fury, this year's summer reading book. I feel a bit light-headed as I knock on the door. Mrs. Hilstone answers, a smile spreading across her face as soon as she sees me. I smile back, my heart warmed by her welcome.

"Hi, Mrs. Hilstone, is Gabe home?"

"Yes, honey, he's right upstairs in his room. Go on up!"

"Thanks so much!" She pats me on the back as I pass her on my way to the stairs.

I try to make as little sound as possible as I approach his room. The door is closed, which helps me maintain the element of surprise. Without thinking, I throw the door open, my arms in the air as if prepared to hug someone.

The word "surprise" catches in my throat when I see Gabe on top of Sophia Freay. His shirt is off, and so is hers. I can't believe my eyes, which makes total sense since I can barely see through the tears. Before either of them can move, I'm already down the stairs and out the door.

I can't keep the sobs from coming out. I'm practically screaming as I run toward my house. I slam the door and run straight to my room, slamming that door too. Flinging myself on my bed, I feel like my heart is physically breaking. The pain in my chest is unbearable, and all I want to do is fall asleep.

I reach my hand out and grab at the snow globe without looking. With my face still firmly planted in the middle of my pillow, I turn the winding key and let the music fill the room. My body relaxes into my bed, and nothing matters anymore.

My eyes are awake before my brain is. They fill with tears before I even have time to open them. Sobs break from my chest, and I bury my head in my pillow

Sonata

to swallow them up, but it doesn't work. The noise deafens me, but I can't keep it in my body; it's escaping my mouth on a mission to let everyone know that my heart is broken. My heart is broken, and it feels different than when my mom died. The pain is radiating to every part of my body, but the funny thing is I can't feel my lips. Right now, I don't even want to think about my lips or whose lips were on them.

I smell her before I see her, and I am instantly calmer. "Honey, what's wrong?" She's sitting on my bed, so I turn over and wrap my arms around her waist as tightly as I can. Stroking my hair, she slides down the bed and hugs me back. "Come on, honey, tell me what's going on."

The tears subside as she wipes them away. "His name is Gabe." She leans back to look at my face. I avoid her eyes, blinking moisture back into mine.

"Please go on, honey." I swallow and finally look her in the eye.

"I thought we had something special; I thought...." I don't want to think about it anymore, but she's looking at me, and all I want to do is tell her all about it. "I thought he felt the same as I do. As I did...I thought I was in love with him."

"Love?!" She practically chokes on the word. I remove myself from her embrace and move to the opposite end of the bed.

"Yes, mother, love. I thought I loved Gabe, was in love with him, and he broke my heart! Please don't give me any of that 'You're too young to know what love is' stuff! I hope I'm wrong! I hope I wasn't in love with him and that someday I will experience real love that I can differentiate from this, but right now my heart hurts, mom!" I clutch at my chest. "It hurts..." The tears are back, and I let them run down my face.

She rolls over, almost flattening me. Rubbing my arms, she says, "I'm sorry, honey. I was just surprised to hear you say that. Of course you can know what love is. Love comes at any age, and you're entitled to feel it when you feel it. As far as this Gabe guy goes - what did he do? How did he break your heart?"

I lay my head on my pillow and sigh, a tear sliding into my ear. "Well, we've been hanging out a lot, going to his friends' parties and talking and stuff." I can feel her nod- ding against my shoulder where she's resting her head.

"Yeah, 'talking'." I roll my eyes and ignore her, continuing.

"Anyway, we've been spending so much time together that when he said he couldn't hang out one night because he had to do summer reading, I thought I'd go over and read with him. I went over to his house, and his mom let me go up to his room. I threw the door open and found him making out with some girl from school."

She's quiet for a long time, and part of me thinks that she's laughing at me in that silent way adults do when they don't want us kids to know that they think we're all just a big joke. I definitely feel like a joke right now, but my heartbreak is no laughing matter.

"I'm sorry, honey. I'm so sorry." That's all she says.

There's not a shred of humor in her voice, only empathy. She kisses my shoulder and lays her head back down. I lean my head on hers, my eyes finally drying. I turn on my side and hug her tightly, burying my face in her chest. She's all I need, and I'm so happy to be back in her arms. As we lay there, motionless, our breathing patterns sync up, and soon we're both asleep in the middle of the day.

CHAPTER TWELVE

It's weird how everything looks the same here in this coma-dream as it does in the real world. When I open the fridge, the same leftover pasta and milk that expired a week ago stare back at me. I grab an orange and peel it on my way to the living room where the same puke green armchair squats in the corner.

I plop down on the couch and shove an orange slice into my mouth, feeling basically over Gabe. I guess grown-ups are right when they say young people don't know what love is. I'm not saying other young people don't know what love is, but I, as a young person, don't feel like I know what love is.

Three oranges later, and I feel completely cleansed of my heartbreak. I'm laughing at the newest episode of Bob's Burgers, I'm playing Candy Crush on my phone, and I'm Facebook stalking some of the girls who just graduated. When my mom walks past, I get

Sonata

really excited. I jump off the couch and run toward her.

"Mom!" I grab her hand and pull her into the living room. "Let's do each other's nails!" She laughs as she lands on the couch.

"It looks like someone is over their first heartbreak." I laugh with her.

"Yes, yes, my heart wasn't broken, whatever." She pats my arm then takes my hand.

"So, what shade were you thinking?"

I can't believe how normal everything feels. As I admire my mom's handy work (pun intended), I can't help but think how I can live here forever. This is the first time I've ever been here two days in a row, and it's pretty amazing. It's like the sun is brighter, the sky is bluer, and the birds aren't rude and chirping all the time. The only thing that's really getting to me is the general loneliness. I love spending time with my mom, but where are all of the other people in the world?

"Mom, I'm going for a walk!"

She meets me at the door, her coat on. "Want me to come?"

Grimacing a bit, I pat her arm and shake my head. "This is something I have to do on my own."

She shakes her head too, rolling her eyes. "You're a weird one, honey."

Rishire Young

Out in this world, I still can't tell the difference. As blue as the sky is, I never noticed it before, so who's to say it's even different. The streets are eerily empty, and I'm starting to think that my mom and I are the only people in this world. Looking at all of the closed doors and shut windows, I'm not sure how I feel about that. The wind blows through my hair, moving around my ears and lifting my arm hairs. I whistle so I feel less alone, but it's haunting, walking around the neighborhood like this. I half expect a lone tumbleweed to roll by or a stray cat to come out of nowhere.

After five blocks, I'm terribly bored and paralyzed by the idea of this being my life in this world. As soon as I get back home, the smell of tacos and guacamole surrounds me.

"Hola!" My mom is wearing the most ridiculous sombrero and the widest grin. "Welcome to my fiesta!"

I roll my eyes and hug her tightly. It's like she's been reading my mind and knows how bored I've been. I walk around her and sniff at the simmering pots and pans holding meats and vegetables. I look back at her and nod. Everything looks great, but a fiesta for two? I don't think that's what the Spanish had in mind.

Sonata

"So, it's just us for this fiesta? Will dad be joining us?" I'm leaning on the counter, trying to look as if that's my idea of a perfect party.

She shakes her head, walking toward me. "No, your dad is working late, but I was thinking you could invite Jordan."

Jordan? Jordan's in this world? Is she different here? Could I really just invite her over? I don't know how anything works here, and I kind of hate it! I reach for the house phone and dial Jordan's number, my fingers stabbing every button. Holding the phone to my ear, I'm surprised to hear it ring like a regular phone. Is it stupid of me to think that everything should be different here?

A few rings in, Jordan answers the phone, startling me out of my reverie. "Hey Nita, what's up?"

I smile just hearing her voice. Things are like they used to be here, and I keep forgetting to feel like I used to, keep forgetting that I don't have to be sad anymore. "Hey! My mom made tacos and burritos, and we're having a fiesta!" I snap my fingers as I say it. "Wanna come over?"

"Of course!"

She's practically here before I can hang up. We hug as soon as she comes inside, and I'm in love with this world all over again - it's like when I first woke up to the sound of my mom's voice. We're laughing as we load our tacos with ground beef, lettuce, and salsa. I shove mountains of guacamole into my mouth before every bite of taco, the ingredients dancing on my tongue, the taco shell falling apart after the first bite. Mom has a Mexican Pandora station playing, and it feels like we're in one of those hokey Tex-Mex places.

After dinner, we play dish Jenga, piling our plates and bowls on top of one another until the whole thing falls. Jordan and I laugh as my mom admits defeat, her guacamole dish toppling the tower. She slaps on dish gloves and gets to work on the pile, while Jordan and I search for a theme-appropriate movie on Netflix. We settle on Casa De Mi Padre, starring Will Ferrell, and wait for my mom to join us on the couch. She plops down, a bowl of buttery popcorn in her lap. We each dig out a handful, munching loudly as the opening sequence begins.

Everything about this day brings me back to a time when I was happy and never even considered the possibility of losing anyone. I'm wired, and all I want to do is stay up and make this day last forever. I can see it in her drooping eyes that my mom doesn't feel the same way. She's yawning as she walks Jordan to the door. Jordan's eyes are barely open as she says goodnight and basically trips out the door. I'm still watch-

Sonata

ing TV, practically bouncing on the couch. I wave my mom over from the stairs where she seems to be hiding.

"Come on, mom! One more movie!" I pat the seat beside me. She drags her feet toward me and slumps into the seat.

"So what will it be? Action, horror, comedy?" I scroll through Netflix excitedly, not even bothering to wait for an answer before I choose a random Kate Hudson movie. I reach over and turn off the lights. Slipping my arm into the crook of my mom's, I lean my head on her shoulder. Before Kate hits the screen, I can hear my mom snoring beside me. I shrug and settle in for the next two hours, my eyes never shifting from the screen.

My leg falls asleep halfway through the movie. I shake it, completely forgetting that my mom is asleep right next to me. She inhales sharply, startled awake by my sudden movement. She pats my leg and moves to stand.

"I think it's time we hit the hay, Honey."

I grab at her hand and try to drag her back down. "But, mom, the movie isn't even over yet, and I'm not tired at all!" I pull my legs to my chest and hug them, looking up at my mom through my eyelashes. She squeezes my arm and shuffles toward the stairs.

Rishire Young

I turn my attention back to the TV till I hear a familiar melody coming toward me. The snowglobe is working its magic on me before I can even see it. My mom puts it on the coffee table and drapes a blanket over me as I lie back on the couch. I know I'm going to wake up in the real world, and I don't really mind. I'm asleep before I can tell my mom I love her, the only regret I can remember as the world goes dark.

There are no harsh fluorescent lights when I open my eyes. I'm wearing my own pajamas, and I'm in my own bed. An IV runs from my arm to a bag filled with a clear liquid, though, just like in the hospital. Another bag dangles by my bedside, filled with the same yellow fluid as before. I don't know how my dad did it, but he's basically turned my room into a hospital room.

My dad pops his head in before opening the door fully. Seeing that I'm awake, he comes to my bedside, kneeling so that we're face-to-face. "Hi, Sweetie. How was your nap?"

Sonata

He doesn't seem nearly as worn out as the first two times I used the snowglobe. I'm sure hearing that these comas aren't life threatening has greatly eased his anxiety. Judging by the still prevalent worry lines on his forehead, it wasn't by much. Since I spent a good chunk of the summer awake, I'm not going to be too concerned.

"It was good. I took a walk, and we had a fiesta with Jordan." I look at him and smile sadly. "I missed you though."

He furrows his eyebrows. "I'm not in this dream world of yours?"

A grimace spreads across my face. "Not so much..."

He rolls his eyes. "Doesn't sound like much of a dream world to me -- more like a nightmare world."

I laugh. "You're right!" I gesture toward the bags of fluids at my side. "How do I get out of this stuff?"

My dad reaches for a medical kit that was stowed underneath my bed. He deftly removes the IV from my arm, placing a bandaid where it once was. I watch in amazement as he works to free me. "Where did you learn how to do all of this?"

He produces a medical waste basket out of nowhere and deposits the needle and empty baggies inside. Without pausing, he says, "I started taking phlebotomy classes after you came home from the hospital the second time. I told you that I was going to do what I needed to do to keep you healthy while you were in your coma over the summer."

He sits on my bed, and we turn to face each other, our eyes not really connecting. There's a war going on in my mind between my guilt at having my dad do all of this just so that I can see my mom and my joy at being able to see my mom. As it has been since I discovered the magic of the snowglobe, my joy wins, so I power through this awkward bit of conversation.

"So what's up? What'd I miss?" Avoiding eye contact, I fiddle with the blanket in my lap.

"Gabe has been coming over a lot, looking for you and asking about you. You should call him."

I push myself off my bed and walk to the window. I peek through the blinds, slitting my eyes toward Gabe's house. My heart races as a shadow passes by his window. Right now, I can't take being so close to him. I have to get out of here, so I gather my towel and head to the bathroom, leaving my dad sitting on my bed.

After a quick shower, I change into a t-shirt and a pair of shorts. I slide on my shoes and head for the front door. My dad appears in the foyer, a questioning look on his face.

"Where are you going, sweetie?"

Sonata

My purse is already slung over my shoulder, and I've already grabbed the door handle. "I'm going to the park. I need to get out of here. I really don't want to see Gabe." He puts his hand on the door, effectively keeping me from opening it.

"What happened with you two? You hadn't used the snowglobe in months, and suddenly you're off in la la land for two weeks. You were so happy this summer, then something changed. What changed, sweetie?"

I lean on the door and look at my dad through teary eyes. "I don't really need to talk about it anymore. That's why I used the snowglobe - to talk to mom. It's just..." I avert my eyes, emotional conversations with my dad about boys not coming easily to me. "Gabe broke my heart, at least I thought he broke my heart, but mom made me realize that I'm fine. I didn't feel for Gabe the way I thought I felt for him, and you don't have to deal with that stuff."

Dad pulls me into a hug and talks into my hair. "Sweetie, I'm glad you were able to talk to your mom about this, but I need you to remember that she's gone. No matter how real your time in that dream world feels, it's not real, and someday it might not exist. You have to learn to come to me with these things just as I have to learn how to talk to you about them."

Rishire Young

I wipe at my eyes and nose with my palm and rub my dad's back. "You're right, but right now, I just need to get out of here." He lets me go, his hand lingering on my shoulder.

I nod and finally head out to my car, not wanting to risk walking to the park for fear that Gabe would catch up with me and trap me in conversation. There's nothing he could say that would erase the image of him kissing another girl. Although I know my heart wasn't really broken, I'm still not ready to just forgive and forget. Once in the car, I roll the windows all the way down and rest my arm in the opening as I drive the ten blocks to the park.

The familiar sight of dancing leaves and laughing children cause tears to well up in my eyes. I half expect to see my mom spinning amongst the leaves, beckoning me to race her. Wandering around aimlessly, I almost lose my way. I find a clearing where a small crowd has gathered to listen to some live music. I peek through them and see a guy around my age strumming an acoustic guitar. He's staring through the crowd, lost in the music he's creating in his head, lost in the moment. His voice lifts above our heads and comes in from every side.

I wander away from the crowd and sit cross-legged on the grass a few yards away, within earshot. I close

Sonata

my eyes and let his soft vocals pass into my ears and down to my heart. I find myself humming along and bobbing my head, loving every sound coming my way. Before I know it, the park is silent. I open my eyes and find that the crowd has dispersed, but the guy is still there, sitting beside his guitar, writing in a notebook. I watch him from where I'm sitting, the thought of approaching him making me nervous yet excited at the same time.

The distance between us seems like a mile. I stand slowly, brushing the loose grass off my butt. Adjusting the straps of my crossbody bag, I walk over to the tree where the guy is sitting. I clear my throat as I approach. He looks up at me, and I almost take a step back, the depth of his green eyes stunning me.

"Uh, hi." He nods but remains silent. "I really loved your music." I'm at a complete loss for words, and I feel like I'm making the worst first impression. Where are my brilliant quips and witty banter? What happened to my brain?

The guy laughs, his attention still on his guitar. My smile feels forced, but I can't keep it off my face. I need to know his name. I don't know what's gotten into me, but I want to know this person. With everything that's happened with Gabe, I don't know why I'm so willing to even think of a guy like this, but I can't help it. Looking at this guy with his shaggy brown hair, evenly tanned skin, and disturbingly deep, green eyes, I can't help it.

"So..." I'm leaning on the tree now, basically looking over his shoulder. "What's your name?"

I feel like the roles have been reversed. I've been relegated to the desperate guy, trying to get a girl's number, and he's the girl who's just too cool to offer it up. I cross my legs at the ankle, trying my hardest to look nonchalant. He finally finishes packing up his guitar and looks up at me from his seat on the floor.

"Dylan."

Ah, one word answers, just what every girl loves. I have no idea how to respond. Should I just offer up my name? Should I leave? He doesn't seem too interested in talking to me, so I should just go. I'm going to go.

"Well...I really enjoyed your music." I kick at the floor and push myself off the tree. I drag my feet as I walk away. It takes everything I have not to grumble to myself as I get farther away. What was I even thinking trying to talk to a guy? Have I not learned my lesson? Am I some sort of masochist?

Just when I start losing all of my self-respect, I hear footsteps behind me. "Hey!" I turn around and see Dylan jogging up to me. "What's your name?"

Sonata

I look him up and down, leaning away from him in true nonchalance. A minute has barely passed, and I've gone from somewhat lovestruck to practically enraged. I don't think this guy deserves to know my name. Where does he get off not giving me the time of day when I ask for it then running me down when I've accepted defeat? As annoyed as I am by his sudden change of heart, I am no jerk, so I answer.

"Nita." I nod then turn to go.

"Wait, Nita."

I stop, not turning around but not completely ignoring him. He walks around to face me. I look up at him, my face stuck in an emotionless expression. He's smiling down at me, a toothy grin that makes me feel things I'm trying hard not to feel. My heart melts a bit, and my anger is replaced with childish infatuation.

"Do you live around here?" The way he bites his lip after asking makes me think that he wants to know more than my address.

This must be how things start - conversations and maybe even relationships. I can't help myself from fast forwarding to a future with this guy - dates in the park, at the movies, having dinner. I take a cursory glance at his lips and decide, yes, those look like kissing lips, full and moisturized. Heat rises to my cheeks, and I find solace in the darkness of my skin. I nod in response to his question. He smiles, forming perfect little dimples in both of his cheeks. I smile back, not too sure where this is going.

"Well, I'm new in town. Would you mind showing me around, maybe taking me to lunch? I'm pretty hungry." He's already sidled up to me and is offering me his arm. I bite my lip and slip my arm into the crook of his. I nod as he leads me toward the parking lot.

CHAPTER THIRTEEN

Lunch is better than I thought it would be. We take separate cars to my favorite Mexican place in town, because, although he's incredibly cute, I'm not trying to get kidnapped and murdered. There we talk non-stop about everything - where he's from, where we go to school, what we want to do when we grow up, what our favorite shows are. Nothing seems off limits, and he's so easy to talk to. It's nothing like it was at the park with both of us doing our little I-don't-care dance. We're both laughing and occasionally touching each other's arms. We share an order of guacamole and chips and each order a beef burrito. I don't even feel awkward eating in front of him - everything is just so easy, and I can't stop smiling.

"So what was up with all that stuff at the park - you ignoring me?" I almost choke on the words.

I don't know what I'm expecting - some sort of explanation that lets me know he feels the same way I do after a short afternoon - and part of me doesn't want to hear what he could have to say, but I'm determined not to treat him like Gabe. I walked on eggshells around Gabe, never wanting to scare him away with my feelings or my confusion, but things feel different with Dylan. I know I'm moving too fast as I'm wont to do, but if there's one thing I know it's that life is too short to move slow.

"Yeah, I was acting like a jerk, I know. I'm sorry..." He looks up at me, head bowed in apology. "It's just, when I saw you coming over, I got a bit nervous. I didn't want to make direct eye contact or say much, cuz I say stupid stuff when I'm nervous. I basically forget the English language when I'm nervous. This is all to say you made me nervous being so bold and cute..." He trails off, averting his eyes and focusing on the mess of chips and guacamole on his plate.

I smile inwardly and outwardly, my whole body buzzing with excitement. Biting my lip, I reach for his hand and tap it lightly. He looks at me and smiles that dimpled smile that I've come to adore. He's reaching for my hand, but I pull back, holding it in my lap.

"You know this isn't a date, right?" He bows his head forlornly. I shake mine furiously. "Oh no! It's not because I don't like you, no no no! It's just you didn't ask me out or anything. This is just two new friends

Sonata

having lunch. If you did ask me out on a date, though, I would say yes."

Our eyes meet, sending my heart into my throat. I swallow but remain silent, determined to give him the space to ask me out. I gave him the perfect set up, now all he has to do is knock it down, that is, if he wants to knock it down.

"You don't say?" I giggle nervously, determined to remain silent, not wanting to step on his asking-me-out-on-a-date toes. "Well, Nita, will you go on a date with me?" He juts his lower lip out, pouting in the cutest way.

I tap my chin and look up at the ceiling as if really giving it some thought. "Hm...I'll have to check my schedule..." I look over at him from the side of my eye, head still tilted upward, giving me quite the angled jawline. He reaches over and slaps me lightly on the arm. I laugh, reaching over and pinching his hand. "Yes, I'll go on a date with you!"

We smile at each other, the world blurring behind him. I rest my head in my palm and continue to stare into his eyes, his stare just as intense. My smile widens, a feat considering how hard I was smiling before. I'm smiling so hard that my eyes are practically closed.

Rishire Young

My phone vibrates in my pocket, breaking my concentration. I pull it out and set it on the table without looking at it. "Maybe we should exchange phone numbers."

Dylan nods, and we pass each other our unlocked phones. Without giving it too much thought, I snap a quick selfie and put it as my profile picture on his phone. I hear my phones' camera click across the table. Looking over, I laugh behind my hand at Dylan's silly expression. We give each other back our phones, our hands brushing during the exchange. I don't want to sound too cliche, but I swear sparks flew, like visible sparks, maybe having something to do with the phones passing each other; I don't know - I'm no scientist!

I look at my phone, a smile frozen on my face. It melts as soon as I see a text from Gabe. "Hey." That's it. Just "Hey". No "Sorry about leading you on for months." or "The kiss you saw meant nothing; my lips are only for you!". Just "Hey.". Where does he get off?

Shaking my head, I turn off my phone and banish all thoughts of Gabe. I smile over at Dylan who had been sitting silently in front of me and reach for my water glass, planning on doing a seductive sip while maintaining eye contact. If I've said it once, I've said it a thousand times, I was not made to flirt. The straw misses my mouth by about a mile, and I'm lucky to have missed my eye, the straw stabbing at the air around my face.

Dylan holds his mouth closed, trying not to laugh. I give up and laugh at myself, the sign of a truly cool girl. He cracks up, gripping my arm, moving his thumb back-and-forth over it. Tingles travel up my arm and down my spine, giving me chills, a feeling I'd never experienced with Gabe.

When I get home, I'm light as a feather. I dance up the stairs to my room and slide onto my bed without disturbing my sheets. I squeeze my eyes shut, flashes of Dylan's face lighting up the darkness. As memories of the last few hours with him play in my mind, I remind myself to reel it in. Everything is going too fast, and I don't want to mess this up the way I messed it up with Gabe. I sit up and drag my knees to my chest, resting my head on them. Running my hands through my hair, I'm lost in thought, racking my brain as to how to proceed with this whole thing. This is still so new to me despite my experience with Gabe, and because of what happened with him, I feel more guarded and scared.

My mind is racing a mile a minute, taking up all of my attention, so much so that I don't notice when my phone buzzes. I dig it out of my back pocket and squint at the too-bright screen. A text from Dylan. I don't know whether to be excited or nervous. We just had the most verbose lunch. What's there to say that hasn't already been said? I tap on the screen to open the message before I can think myself into a stupor.

"I had a great time with you today. Can we schedule that date for tomorrow night? Dinner? I know of this amazing Thai place down the street from my apartment. What do you say?" I can't keep the smile from spreading across my face. I read then reread the message, not wanting to respond too quickly.

After an appropriate five minutes, I tap out a short but sweet reply. "I love Thai food! Just tell me when and where and I'll be there!" I hit send as soon as the message is crafted, not giving myself time to regret the exclamation points.

My phone vibrates before I can put it down. "I'll pick you up at 7. What's your address?" I bite my lip, unsure as to whether or not I should give this near stranger my address. I shrug and decide there could be no harm in it, typing in the address and hitting send.

In no time I'm ready for bed, my pajamas giving me the freedom that my jeans did not. Closing my eyes, I let the day wash over me. I want to dream about today, relive every moment I shared with Dylan. I bury myself deep in the pillows and pull the comforter over

Sonata

my head. The air gets stuffy, and I'm surrounded by my own scent. The warmth is delicious and sends me right to sleep with dreams of tomorrow's date dancing in my head.

I can't get out of bed fast enough - I'm so excited for tonight. I've showered and brushed my teeth before my father has even put on a pot of coffee.

"Good morning, father." I dance up to him and plant a light kiss on his cheek. He looks at me quizzically, his head cocked to the side and his eyebrows furrowed. I give him a quick hug before taking a seat at the dining room table. Clasping my hands on top of the table, I blink up at my dad. "So what's for breakfast?"

He wipes his hands on a towel and walks toward me. "What's got you so chipper this morning? Furthermore, what has you awake?"

I shrug and roll my eyes. "It's a beautiful day! Do I have to have a reason to enjoy the day?" He laughs and pats my knee.

"No, honey, it's just a bit out of character for you!" I put my hand to my chest and feign indignation.

"I take offense to that." He messes with my hair and walks back to the stove.

Swinging my legs, I hum a little tune, not realizing it's the same tune my mom was humming my first trip to the dream world. I smile at myself, the memory lifting and breaking my heart at the same time. My dad brings breakfast to the table and we share a meal like we haven't in a long time - talking with our mouths full, throwing our heads back in laughter, and sitting at the table longer than the meal lasts. This day has started off amazingly, and I'm sure tonight will support that amazing-ness.

Full on eggs and bacon, I go back upstairs to my room and grab a magazine off my dresser. Flipping through the pages, I feel like an absurdly regular girl, like one of those girls you see on TV who chills in her room reading instead of watching the very TV that she's on. I don't usually read magazines as evidenced by my huge stack of them on my dresser dating back to last summer. After breakfast, I usually settle into the little dent in the couch that has formed from me sitting in it so much and switch on the TV armed with enough water and snacks to last me the afternoon. I guess this whole snowglobe-Gabe-Dylan-thing has made me a whole new person!

Sonata

I breeze through three issues of Elle magazine before I get out of bed. My limbs feel a bit stiff, and there's a spot on my back that I can't reach that's aching slightly, but I feel like it's been an afternoon well spent. After cracking my back, I dig my cell phone out from under my mattress where I forgot I lodged it this morning.

Air hitches in my throat when I see that Dylan has texted me. I can't help but think he's bailing on tonight. My hand shakes as I click the message open. I release the breath I didn't realize I was holding when I see the litany of smiley face emojis that fill my screen. Smiling, I tap out a reply that's just a row of winky face emojis. I chew my lower lip as I watch the three dots dance at the bottom of the screen.

"You've got quite a way with words, Nita."

Heat rises to my face as my fingers fly across the screen. This witty banter is getting me more and more excited for tonight. We go back-and-forth almost unceasingly for a solid hour, all the while I'm running around my room trying to pick out an outfit that's the perfect combination of cute and casual. The way we can text in such a seamless manner plants the seed of a silly thought in my head, a thought I barely want to acknowledge because it's so ridiculous and childish, and I feel like I'm jumping the gun - but we were made for each other.

We fit like puzzle pieces, and I get a bad taste in my mouth just thinking about it. This comfort that I feel scares me, reminds me of how I felt with Gabe, and we all know how that turned out. I'm dangerously close to daydreaming a future with Dylan, and that can't be good. It's like whenever I tell someone about something that hasn't happened yet or I imagine how things might end up, nothing ever goes as planned. I need to do something to get my mind off of him.

"Dad?" I run down the hallway to my dad's room and knock on the door. "Are you busy?" I shift my weight from my heels to my toes as I wait for his reply. His footsteps shake the floor as he approaches the door. He opens it a crack and peeks his head out.

"What's up, sweetie?" I lean into the doorframe and peer behind him into his room.

"What are you doing? Is there something going on in your room?" He laughs and opens the door all the way.

"No, silly, I just didn't think we were going to be having a full on conversation." He waves his arm Vanna White style. "Come on in."

My eyebrows furrow as I pass him into the room. I plop down into his armchair and cross my legs at the

Sonata

ankles, making myself comfortable. "So, what's up?" He joins me in the corner of the room, sitting in the adjacent armchair.

"Can't a daughter want to hang out with her father?" He looks at me with slightly widened eyes, his eyebrows raised to his hairline.

"Don't you have a date tonight?" A grimace works its way across my face.

"How did you know that?" He shrugs, leaving it at that. I roll my eyes and leave it at that. Two can play that game!

"Are you going to tell me what's up or not?" I laugh, not really knowing how to answer. Minutes go by in silence, the space between us lengthening. My dad rubs his eyes and sighs. "Alright, have it your way. I assume you're just killing time before your date, so let me take this opportunity to talk to you about safe sex." I almost spit out the saliva collecting on my tongue, gagging on the collection in my esophagus.

"Dad, no, I don't need that talk." I shake my head vigorously as I stand.

"Oh no," he says as he blocks my path to the door. "You came in here and interrupted me, so now you have to listen to me talk. Sit back down, young lady." Still shaking my head, I back into the chair. He sits down and rests his chin in the palm of his hand.

Rishire Young

"Now where to begin...?" I sink into the chair and cover my face, one eye uncovered to watch the clock.

The sound of tires crunching up the driveway quickens my heart rate. I look out the window and catch a glimpse of Dylan walking toward the front door. Throwing things into my purse, I run out of my bedroom and fly down the stairs. I have the door open before Dylan's long, slender finger can enter the doorbells' airspace.

"Whoa!" He takes a step back, his finger still hovering in the air. "Hey there. Someone's jumpy." He smiles that smile that I can't stop thinking about. I blink a few times to settle myself and inhale deeply before opening my mouth to speak. I laugh, a sound that's a bit higher than I expected and shriller than I wanted. He keeps smiling, the sides of his mouth twitching ever so slightly as the muscles in his face begin to strain.

"So, do you want to head out?" I already have the door closed behind me. I walk toward him, my arm poised to take its place in the crook of his. Everything falls into place as we walk to his car. I resist the urge

Sonata

to lean my head on his shoulder in a remake of a romantic comedy scene.

His car is a little older than mine and a bit rough around the edges; it's exactly the car I had imagined he would have when I first met him in the park, a car with character that looks like it's been through some stuff and has some interesting stories to tell. The leather seats are worn and comfortable, cradling my butt as soon as it makes impact. The radio is a newer version that I can tell didn't come with the car.

"I take it you really like music." I've never been one for car conversations, but things come so easily when I'm with Dylan. He's so new and interesting, and I have so many questions that I can turn into comments that make me sound observant, or at least that's how I hope they make me sound.

"You noticed the new radio, huh?" He pokes it, turning on some soft rock - a song I don't recognize.

"Ha, yeah, one of these things is not like the other." He pinches my shoulder, and I swat his hand away. He turns up the volume and looks at me from the corner of his eye for a second, returning his gaze to the road like a good driver.

"Do you know this song?" I wrack my brain to see if somewhere in its deepest recesses I have some unknown knowledge of soft rock that I can impress him with. No such luck.

"Sorry to say I don't. I like it, though." And I'm not even lying. It's the perfect song to set the mood for this car ride - soft and sweet and beautiful.

"I've got a lot to teach you, then." It sounds flirty and suggestive and just the tiniest bit dirty. I smile to myself, playing it cool by not looking at him. He laughs, turns up the volume a bit more, and taps his fingers on the steering wheel as we drive out of my neighborhood and toward the city.

The music fills the car, making the silence comfortable and noisy. I rest my head on my hand and stare out the window, watching the scene change from suburban to urban, daydreaming about future me moving out of my dad's house and living on my own in the city. Before I know it, we're at the restaurant, and I quickly realize that my stomach has been trying to eat itself.

As soon as we step into the restaurant, I'm immediately transported by the scents that greet me. The lights are dim by the tables, a small candle the only thing to see by. We are seated immediately, because we have a reservation - I've never felt so mature in my life. Dylan holds the chair out for me and pushes me in like real gentlemen do on TV. We open our huge

Sonata

menus and read silently, every dish sounding delicious beyond measure.

I peek over my menu at Dylan who's doing the same. We laugh when our eyes meet and set our menus down to look at each other. "Do you want to split an appetizer?" I nod and only let half of my mouth smile, something I'm sure he doesn't notice in the dim lighting. "What are you thinking?" I'm in no position to make any decisions right now, so I just shrug.

"Everything looks so good. I'll be fine with anything." He laughs and lifts his eyes, making eye contact with our server and calling her over.

We don't order our entrees until after we've finished our appetizer. We wipe the plate clean, using small chunks of pork shumai as sponges to soak up the remaining sweet peanut sauce. Our entrees are at our table in minutes, the speedy service one of my favorite things about Thai restaurants. I deeply inhale the steam coming off my Kee Mao, feasting my eyes on the large noodles and tofu squares. Dylan's Pad Thai looks good too. We ask for extra plates so we can each try the other's food.

The conversation is as free flowing as the water, only stopping when we shove forkfuls of noodles in our mouths. I'm laughing every five minutes, everything Dylan says as funny as a Judd Apatow movie. There's a lot of touching, nothing too crazy - a graze there, a squeeze here, our knees constantly hitting each other under the table. As far as dates go, I'm sure this is the best one in the history of ever.

As people leave and our water glasses get refilled once, twice, a thousand times, Dylan and I don't move. Neither of us get up to go to the bathroom, and our eyes never leave each others'. From the outside I'm sure we look like we're in love, and on the inside, I'm definitely feeling it. The way he's looking at me, I'm sure he feels the same...At least I hope he feels the same.

The lights dim around us. The check has been sitting on the table for about a half hour, and my mind is going a mile a minute - thinking about whether or not I should grab for the check, thinking about Dylan's impenetrably dark eyes, thinking that I need to blink more before my eyes dry out. Waiters hover around our table, trying not to look like they're rushing us.

"Would you two like any dessert?" Her grin looks forced, and I would feel bad for her if I wasn't having so much fun. Dylan nods in the waiter's direction without taking his eyes off mine. We both pass up our dessert menus and order the cheesecake. I can almost

Sonata

hear the waiter cursing us as she heads to the kitchen with our orders.

"I think she's going to spit in our cake." I laugh, a light, airy sound that's foreign to my mouth.

"Should we cancel our order?" He asks. I frown, my eyes going wide and puppy-dog-like. "Ha I'll take that as a no. I'm sure we'll barely be able to taste the spit." I reach across the table and pinch him.

"Ew! That's disgusting!"

"Hey, that hurt!" He rubs the hand that I pinched dramatically. "It's true; you can barely taste spit!"

Our cheesecakes come, and he's right, I can't taste the spit at all. We talk about it the whole ride back to my house. We laugh above the radio, and when he parks in my driveway, we can't figure out how to say goodbye. He turns off the engine, and shifts in his seat, facing me. I do the same, leaning forward a bit so that our faces are about a foot apart.

He inches forward, resting his elbows on that armrest thing between the driver and passenger seats - whatever that's called. We meet above it, our noses connecting before our lips do. He smiles against my lips, interrupting the kiss. I laugh into his mouth, the taste of our cheesecakes mingling.

"I'm going to say this one more time - you were so right - I could only taste the cheesecake during that kiss, no spit at all!" His laugh comes out in a sort of howl that takes me off guard.

"Nita, you're killing me! I've got to get home, but you're making me want to stay!" I screw up my face and poke out my neck.

"How's this?" Cocking my head to the side, I stick out my tongue and scrunch up my nose. "Does this make you want to leave?"

Dylan strokes my cheek, his eyes softening. "Quite the opposite," he says, smiling with only his eyes. "I really like you, Nita, and I think this is going to be fun."

CHAPTER FOURTEEN

The next day, Dylan shows up at my house unannounced, a pair of rollerblades on his finger, dangling by their laces. I look at him with raised eyebrows. "Do you expect me to wear those?"

He laughs, the sound tickling my eardrums. "Are you saying you don't know how to skate?"

I snatch the skates from him and turn on my heel, heading up the stairs. "I didn't say anything of the sort. I assure you I can skate circles around you."

"I'd like to see you try!" He calls up from just inside the front door.

I stop at the top of the stairs and turn to him. "Aren't you coming up?" He shakes his head. "Why not?" I let the rollerblades swing beside me as I lean on the banister.

He mimics the move at the bottom of the stairs and shrugs. "It wouldn't be very appropriate for me to be in your room after just one date." A smirk plays across my face, and I shrug back, continuing my walk to my bedroom.

Once inside, a grin breaks my face wide open. I really like that he's not up here right now, pressuring me to perform just with his presence. I like that he's respecting me in a way that Gabe never did, in a way that I didn't realize I wanted to be respected. I guess when he said that this is going to be fun, he meant good, old fashioned, wholesome fun, like rollerblading in the park fun. Thinking about it now, it's just the kind of fun that I'm looking for.

I grab a pair of socks and sneakers and run down the stairs. Dylan is leaning on the closed front door, his gaze wandering from surface to surface, taking in his surroundings. I sit on the last step and slide on my socks and sneakers.

"You're not going to wear the blades?" He motions to his own pair on his feet that look comfortably worn in.

"Oh, no. I would bust my butt if I tried to rollerblade in the street."

Dylan throws his head back and lets out the howl that I heard last night. It cracks me up, and soon we're both howling. "So what was all that talk about skating circles around me?"

Sonata

I shrug, something that I've taken to doing a lot recently. "Just that - talk."

Sticking out my tongue, I push him away from the door and fling it open. He slides toward the living room before he catches himself and goes after me. We head to the park at a brisk pace, me practically running to keep up with him on his wheels. He skates backwards and sticks his tongue out at me as we get close to the entrance.

I smirk and raise my eyebrows, a sense of competition forming in my gut. Once inside the park gates, I stop at the nearest bench and put my rollerblades on. I tie my sneakers' laces together and hang them around my neck. Dylan does some spin moves in the distance, no doubt trying to impress me. I watch as he glides effortless, my mouth ticking up at the corners. Mission accomplished.

Despite his clear skating prowess, we just slide through the park together. There's no fancy footwork or races, just a casual stroll on wheels. He doesn't even try to hold my hand, instead opting to keep his in his pockets the whole time. I'm grateful to have my hands free as I nearly fall every five minutes. I see him stifle fits of laughter out of the corner of my eye. Doing him a favor, I laugh at myself, something I feel like I've been doing a lot since I met him.

Rishire Young

It's an easy, breezy day, and I come home content. The summer is winding down nicely, and it's a relief after having spent so much time with a guy that I can no longer stand thinking about.

At my front door, Dylan and I sit on the steps, a light sheen of sweat illuminating our foreheads. I unlace the rollerblades and hand them to him. "How did you know my size?"

He messes around with the laces and shrugs. "I was hoping you'd be the same size as my sister. It would've been really awkward if you weren't."

Making eye contact, he laughs then bites his lower lip. He looks like he wants to kiss me but is trying to talk himself out of it. I can see the wheels spinning in his head as his eyes move from my lips to my eyes and back.

I giggle gently then reach for the back of his head, pulling him into me. Our lips meet, and it feels like a reunion. He sighs into my mouth, the exhalation filling my lungs with his breath. I scoot closer to him as the kiss intensifies. A loud cough pulls us apart.

Jordan stands over us, a thinly veiled smile playing at her lips. I roll my eyes and laugh as I reach for her hand. She helps me up, and I pat at my butt to get the dirt off. Dylan stands next to me, smiling at Jordan.

"Hey, Jordan. What are you doing here?"

Sonata

Without taking her eyes off of Dylan, she sidles up to me and whispers, "Who is this?"

I shake my head, rolling my eyes again. Motioning to Dylan, I say, "This is Dylan. We met at the park a few days ago. We just got back from rollerblading."

Jordan waggles her eyebrows. "So that's what the kids are calling it these days."

Dylan nearly chokes on his laughter. I shove Jordan lightly, a giggle pushing through my lips. "You're such a dork."

Dylan puts a hand on my shoulder and motions toward his car. "I'm gonna head home. See you later?" I nod, biting my lip as the kiss we just shared plays back in my mind. He stares at the ground for a beat, a blush creeping up his neck. "It was nice to meet you Jordan."

"You too!" Jordan waves as Dylan slides into his front seat. We watch as he backs out of the driveway then turn back to each other.

Jordan's mouth is forming an O and her eyebrows have become one with her hairline. "Who are you?! Two boys in one summer?! That has to be a world record!"

I wince not wanting to give Gabe even one second of thought. "What's up? Why'd you come over?" At the hurt look on Jordan's face, I add, "I mean, not that I mind! I was totally going to call you when I got back, so this really just saves me some minutes, as unlimited as they are."

She smiles, a sigh rushing out of her. "I just wanted to remind you about Jackie's party tomorrow. You're still coming right?"

I nod. "Wouldn't miss it for anything in this world."

She elbows me playfully. "You should bring Dylan."

I swat at her arm. "I've only known him for, like, three days. You meeting him now was mere coincidence."

"Are you saying that you were going to hide him from me?"

My face screws up in thought. I hadn't really thought about introducing Dylan to my friends, well, my friend. It wasn't something I had to do with Gabe since we go to the same school and pretty much know all of the same people. With Dylan going to a different school, I could have kept him all to myself forever. What's the point of sharing something that could end with a snap?

That thought weighs me down, so I sit back on the steps. Jordan joins me, her hand making its way to my shoulder. "What's going on in that head of yours, Nita?"

Sonata

I sigh, the thought of rehashing what happened with Gabe again making my head hurt. "I was just thinking about what happened with Gabe - how I caught him making out with Sophia after he had been so sweet to me. How could I have been so wrong about him? And if I was wrong about him, I could be wrong about anyone."

Jordan shakes her head, an angry look in her eyes. "I can't believe he did that. Why didn't you tell me?"

I shrug. "As soon as it happened, I used the snow-globe."

A sad smile crosses Jordan's face. I avert my eyes, my gaze landing on my sneakers, their loose laces reminding me of rollerblading a few hours ago. I almost don't want to get into the whole Gabe thing with Jordan, especially since I saw her in the dream-coma the day after I got over it, which almost makes it feel like I have already told her. That second day felt more real than the other days, and that's a bit scary. What if I go into the dream-coma, and it feels so real that I never get out of it? If Jordan was there the last time, who could show up next? Gabe? Dylan? My dad?

I feel like if he were ever there, I would never leave. Why would I when I would have everything I could ever want? I would have both of my parents and my best friend. At that point, what would this world even have to offer me? Heartbreak? Hard pass.

As I'm stuck in my reverie having completely forgotten about Jordan, my dad pulls into the driveway. Watching him get out of the car, I realize what I would lose if I gave up this world, or more accurately, who I would hurt. This whole time I had been using the snowglobe to make myself feel better, not caring that it was breaking my dad's heart to see me like that - in a coma. I know that this is taking a toll on him, but somehow it's just hitting me how selfish I've been.

He clicks the door shut and waves over at us. Jordan stands, waving back. I get to my feet and rush toward him. He's taken aback by my hug, but gathers himself in time to squeeze me back.

"What's all this about?"

I lean back and smile up at him. "Welcome home, dad."

He smiles down at me, tears filling his eyes as he takes me in. I'm sure he can see right through me, see through to the part of me that is still broken, to the part of me that constantly aches, to the part of me that feels the way he feels.

It's weird, but since I've lost my mom, I've only been thinking of her as my mom, but she wasn't just my mom. She was his wife, too, and he's grieving just

Sonata

as much as I am. That thought pierces my heart, because I know it means the end. It means that I have to say goodbye to the one thing that has been keeping my grief at bay, because it has also been exacerbating his.

A single tear runs down my cheek. My dad wipes it away with his thumb. Jordan makes a small noise behind us, having been completely forgotten. We laugh at ourselves, looking like sad sacks on the front lawn. I put my arm around my dad and Jordan as we walk into the house.

That night, I treat them to the same fiesta I had with my mom that second day in the dream-coma. We watch Casa De Mi Padre and play dish jenga, which I lose on purpose. As I wash the dishes, I can't help but think about everything that has happened this summer. I was more social and active these past few months than I have been since my mom died. It was like I was the old me again, the me before the grief and the seemingly unending pain. Sure, that me only really hung out with Jordan, but it was more than I had allowed myself to do after the accident.

Once it sunk in that my mom was never going to come back and that life can really end in the blink of an eye, I couldn't get myself to care about anything. I mean, what's the point when everything ends eventually. Life, love, happiness - nothing lasts forever. I turn to watch Jordan and my dad set up Monopoly on the coffee table. Seeing them laughing as they choose their little game pieces, I know that a moment with the people I love is more than enough. I've been stealing more moments with my mom while robbing my dad of moments with me, and I know now that it's not right. I don't know how I'm going to get through this grief without the dream-coma, but I do know that I have to find a way, for my dad's sake. I also know that I will, with his and Jordan's help.

I dry my hands on a dish towel and skip over to the couch. "Are you two ready to lose?" My dad and Jordan exchange a look that says "Yeah right". I roll my hands and snatch up the thimble piece. "Whatever! Monopoly's not my game, but I sure do love playing!"

It's been a while since I've been this naturally tired, and I'm sure it has something to do with rollerblading this morning and having a stomach full of beef and cheese. I wave at Jordan as she makes her way down the street then turn to slink up the stairs. My bed is so comfortable that I almost forget to turn on the snow-

Sonata

globe. Within seconds, I have succumbed to the sweet relief of sleep.

It feels like it's been such a long time since I've been here despite the fact that it looks just like the home I left last night. I lie in bed awake, not wanting to do what I know I have to do. I have to end this, and I know it's going to hurt like crazy. For a split second, I think that I can just let today be a normal day in this dream-coma. My mom and I can go to the park and watch movies, and nothing has to seem like it's going to change. Even as I think it, I know that wouldn't be the best way to do this. I have a chance to do something that I didn't get to do a year ago - say goodbye to my mom.

As soon as I catch sight of her in the kitchen, I start to think of how strange this has all been - a different strange than the obvious strange of an alternate universe brought about by a snowglobe. With all of my memories of my time here as well as the time I spent with my mom when she was actually alive, I don't really feel like she's gone. Sometimes I have to consciously remind myself that she is, but even then it's no big deal. It's like I've completely stopped mourning her, and that breaks my heart.

Walking toward her, I can't stop the tears from soaking my face. As soon as she sees me, she rushes to me and wraps me in her arms. I bury my head in her shoulder and let out a body convulsing sob. I shake as she sits me down at the dining table. She pulls up a chair beside me and strokes my hand as I quiet down.

"What's going on, honey?" There's always something going on when I come here. My trips to this "other world" are always so loaded that I'm surprised I've been able to enjoy myself. I look deep into my mom's eyes and feel all the life leave my body.

"Mom, you're dead." Fresh tears fill my eyes, and it feels like my insides have crumbled. "I don't know how to explain this to you - I don't even understand it myself - but this is a dream. I'm dreaming, and I've been having this dream for a while now, but this isn't real." I watch as her expression doesn't change, as she just looks at me, bathed in motherly love. "You died in a plane crash about a year ago."

Sonata

She reaches over and rubs my back. "Honey, I know." My mouth nearly drops open. She pulls me into a hug and continues to rub my back. "I know, but I don't know know, you know?" She releases me and gestures around the kitchen. "I didn't think all of this was real. Where's your father? Where are all of the people? None of it made sense, but I knew this was all for you." She takes my hand in hers and squeezes gently. "I'm here for you, honey." Her smile is so soft that it's almost a frown. "I always will be, but you've got to live."

I open my mouth to speak, to interrupt this train of thought, argue against this idea that what I'm doing here isn't living, but she interrupts me with a quickness. "No, honey, listen - this isn't a life, you dreaming and remaining in this realistic denial. I know it's hard, but you have to wake up. You have to get through this and be stronger for it." With her hand on my cheek, she stands and hovers over me.

"Everything happens for a reason, and you need to give my death a reason. Live with the love we've shared and share that love with the people in your life who are alive." I stand despite how unsteady I feel. I'm beyond speechless, but I know what she's saying is true. "Feel free to remember the times we shared here, but remember that they weren't real and that the real memories are inside of you." She pulls me in and hugs me with all of her might. With every ounce of strength I have, I hug her back. "Take this as the goodbye I wasn't able to say," she whispers in my ear. "Goodbye, my sweet, sweet girl. I love you so much."

My eyes are dry, but a single tear escapes as I squeeze them shut. "I love you too, mom. Goodbye."

Somehow I'm awake and in the real world without having used the snowglobe. On the wall across from my bed, I see the calendar with a large red circle around tomorrow - the first day of school. I was only out for two days, which makes me think that the magic has faded. I've missed Jackie's party and have spent most of the summer leading myself to a false heartbreak. Groaning, I cover my head with my comforter and settle back into bed. It's like everything is happening all over again - my mom is dying all over again - and I can't face it. Not again. Not after being

Sonata

able to touch her, talk to her, be with her. How can I go back?

I throw the covers off and reach for the snowglobe. Looking into the hard plastic encased dome, I know it's over. I can't go back, because it won't be the same. Something has changed in that world, and for all I know, my mom won't be there anymore. I've fully awoken from the dream, and it's as if the snowglobe has shattered.

Tracing the sphere, I wonder if I should do just that - shatter the snowglobe. Although I can never have the same dream again, I can't imagine destroying this symbol of magic, of an alternate reality where things were okay. This snowglobe will forever remind me of the time I got my mom back, the time I got to say goodbye. I can't destroy that.

My body grows heavy just thinking of our last minutes together. I turn the snowglobe over and remove the batteries. Throwing the batteries into my nightstand drawer, I place the snowglobe back on the table and settle back into bed. Today's the last day of summer, and all I want to do is stay in bed and not think about anything - not Dylan or Gabe or school or the life my mom wants me to live filled with the purpose of her death and the vitality of knowing I could die at any minute just as she did. I may have been "asleep" this past year, but today I actually want to sleep.

When I wake up, I feel ready to do what I have to do - to feel happy in the face of my grief, interact with my peers, and make the most of what I've got. Wasting the last few minutes before my alarm goes off, I switch on my phone and check my messages. A few missed calls from Jordan and a few texts from Dylan that I take my time reading and responding to. I haven't been thinking of him much in the last few days, but now that I am, I miss him.

"I miss you. Can you hang out tonight?" I set my phone down and undress, wrapping my robe around me tightly. The cotton caresses my bare skin, and I'm awash in comfort. My phone buzzes right before I leave for the bathroom.

Dylan - "I'd love to."

My heart lifts, and I'm filled with an excitement for this new thing. Looking over at the snowglobe as the sun hits it through the slats in my blinds, illuminating it in an ethereal way that reminds me of the magic it allowed me to experience, I can't help but think that things are actually going to be okay - I'm going to miss my mom like crazy, but I can get through this, and she'll be with me the whole way.

ABOUT THE AUTHOR

Rishire Young is an author, actress, and professional daydreamer. At the age of 15, she lost her mother and twin sister in a tragic car accident and has been working through her grief ever since. By speaking at youth grief retreats and contributing to a book about grief, Rishire finds meaning in her mourning. After graduating from New York University with a Bachelor's in Music, having majored in music business and minored in creative writing, she settled in Brooklyn, NY. Rishire loves to read, write, and try new things. She enjoys exploring different New York City neighborhoods as well as checking out new restaurants around the city. When she's not spending time with her head in a book, she is hanging out with her godchildren or watching a bunch of TV.

Milton Keynes UK
Ingram Content Group UK Ltd.
UKHW050733180724
445674UK00016B/609